Jeet's eyes got that glazed-over look that they get when he's protecting himself from excessive horse talk. "Robin," he said, "no one here is interested in horses. Of all the things they've approached me about covering, horses was not one of them."

"Well, I could do other stuff," I said, a wee sullen note creeping into my voice.

"And it's *whom*, not *that*," Jeet said.

"Huh?"

"A woman *whom* I met, not a woman *that*—"

But I was saved by the tapping on the driver's-side window that DeWitt had undertaken.

Jeet took a long, deep sigh and turned the engine—and thus the air-conditioning in the car—off. He saved us from suffication, however, by rolling the window down. A cloud of hot, sticky air moved in at once. I could feel my hair going limp and my skin getting damp.

DeWitt hunched over, wide-eyed. "Got to talk to you, Jeet," he said, dropping an age-freckled hand over Jeet's forearm. There was a note of urgency in his voice. "Someplace private. No fooling, boy. This is big."

By Carolyn Banks:

TART TALES: Elegant Erotic Stories
PATCHWORK
THE GIRLS ON THE ROW
THE DARKROOM
MR. RIGHT
THE ADVENTURES OF RUNCIBLE SPOON
THE HORSE LOVER'S GUIDE TO TEXAS
    (coauthor)
A LOVING VOICE: A Caregiver's Book of Read-
    Aloud Stories for the Elderly (coeditor)
A LOVING VOICE II: A Caregiver's Book of More
    Read-Aloud Stories for the Elderly
    (coeditor)
DEATH BY DRESSAGE*
GROOMED FOR DEATH*
MURDER WELL-BRED*
DEATH ON THE DIAGONAL*

*Published by Fawcett Books

DEATH ON THE DIAGONAL

Carolyn Banks

FAWCETT GOLD MEDAL • NEW YORK

A Fawcett Gold Medal Book
Published by Ballantine Books
Copyright © 1996 by Carolyn Banks

All rights reserved under International and Pan-American Copyright Conventions. Published in the United States by Ballantine Books, a division of Random House, Inc., New York, and simultaneously in Canada by Random House of Canada Limited, Toronto.

http://www.randomhouse.com

Library of Congress Catalog Card Number: 95-96173

ISBN 0-449-14968-4

Manufactured in the United States of America

First Edition: July 1996

10 9 8 7 6 5 4 3 2

For Paula Tremblay, my true blue friend,
and Elvis, her equine companion.

I want to thank Davis McAuley; my editor, Elisa Wares; and my agent, Vicky Bijur, for reading this manuscript so carefully and for giving me some great suggestions. I also want to thank that fine competitor Pam Goodrich. She uttered the wonderful line about the Uzi (attributed to Tiny here) when she came to Shiron Farms to give a clinic.

CHAPTER 1

I'm ashamed to say it, but the first thing out of my mouth was, "What about our horses?"

And when you hear the circumstances, you'll understand why I say "ashamed." We were in a rental car, on our way to Bucking Hill Cemetery in Bead, Texas. In a procession with our headlights on. Three cars behind the hearse. Said hearse bearing one of Jeet's boyhood chums, Townsend Loving, like Jeet, age thirty-eight.

It had pretty much floored Jeet when he'd heard, but now he was saying that Della Loving had cornered him at the funeral parlor and asked him to take over the weekly newspaper Towns had owned and edited until she could find someone else.

It would mean me going back home alone, packing and FedEx-ing Jeet's necessities, and then hying it on down to Bead myself, to live for weeks or months, who knows how long.

This prospect did not exactly incite my glee.

"I just can't see how I can tell her no," Jeet was saying, "especially since she knows I'm on leave."

Jeet's a newsman himself, the food critic for the _Austin Daily Progress_, but he'd been given a year's leave of absence—at no pay, of course—in order to write a book about the foods he'd grown up with. The publisher's advance had been paltry, but we

1

figured we could scrabble by. Then we learned we got only half of the money when Jeet signed the contract and the rest when he finished the manuscript.

It had been a helluva two months so far.

"Della says she'll pay me by the week," Jeet said. This was evidently the carrot and a mighty big one it was, too. Still, that was when I'd uttered my remark.

"We'll take the horses with us," he assured me. "How hard can it be to find someone to take them in?"

"Boarding horses," I told him, "costs an arm and a leg."

"I'm not talking about some swanky place with an indoor arena, Robin," Jeet was saying. "I'm talking about some farmer's field. A what-do-you-call-it?"

Jeet isn't very horsey or, if you want to really get down to it, countrified. This, despite having grown up in Abilene. "Pasture?" I tried.

"Pasture, right. So what do you say?" He glanced over at me.

I didn't say anything. I was imagining said pasture, all rocks and hillocks. Its century-old cedar posts would list perilously, inviting the horses to step to the other side, where rattlesnakes and scorpions would no doubt be lying in wait.

I didn't say that. Instead, I tried, "We'll have to rent a place for ourselves. And make our mortgage payment on the farm besides. I don't see how—"

The car jolted to a stop and I looked up to see the widow, Della, being helped out of the long black Cadillac limo immediately behind the hearse.

Della was younger than I was, but she didn't look it right then. Right then she could have passed for my mother and, indeed, was dressed pretty much the way my mother would have been dressed, very sleek and stylish in a black linen sheath. Of course, it's hard not to look sleek and stylish in a black linen sheath, particularly when your body is shaped the way Della's was shaped.

Perfectly. We're talking the proverbial hourglass here. But then, Della had been the campus beauty when she'd met and married Towns.

She didn't seem to have changed. Not a speck of flab on her body or even so much as a crinkly little laugh line on her expertly made-up face. (I don't know about you, but I had them—said lines—in my early twenties, spiderweb crevices in the corners of my eyes.)

Anyway, Jeet was looking at Della, too. He wasn't assessing her charms, though, I could tell. Jeet, if you want to know, is pretty much impervious to such things.

No kidding. One time at a party a woman was flirting with him, going on and on about her sunburn and pulling the neckline of her dress down farther and farther as she talked so that Jeet could see. Jeet was concentrating on one of the hors d'oeuvres, however. He was frowning, I later learned, because he thought the chef had overdone the anchovy paste.

Anyway, here was this woman, displaying more and more cleavage to no avail. She stopped just short of topless and, I understand, took the whole thing pretty personally, opting for saline implants shortly thereafter (although if she'd have asked me, I'd have gladly explained my husband's priorities).

But this is beside the point. Because right now Jeet was saying, "Every cent that Della and Towns had is invested in that little newspaper. She has to keep it going. She'll start running an ad for a regular editor right away, though, so figure two or three months at most."

Two or three months!

But I was watching her and imagining myself in the same boat, a young widow. And also, I was remembering Jeet's face when he'd picked up the tele-

phone and heard about Towns's death. So I forbade
the image of my horses shying as tumbleweed rolled
toward them—I mean, I hadn't seen any tumbleweed,
but wouldn't a place like this have it?—from entering
my mind. I swallowed. "All right, let's do it," I said.

Jeet looked over at me, took my hand, and
squeezed it. I'm not sure he would have if he'd
known how much I'd wanted to say no. I mean, I
like the life we have. Like our little Primrose Farm
and living close to Austin. Like having my best
friend, Lola, right next door to ride with and talk to.
Like having my horses, Plum and Spier, right outside my door. Like trailering them to lessons
at Wanda's and clinics and schooling shows. God, at
this point, I even liked the wrangling at our local
dressage club over how we're going to spend our ac-
cumulated dues.

What did Bead have that could compare with
that? Nothing, I was sure. I'd probably be lucky to
find a couple of trails to clomp around on.

I smiled weakly and, I hoped, bravely, and then
we were getting out of the car.

The air-conditioned car. Which made the air outside feel like a warm, wet washcloth. Bead was about
eighty miles from where we live, which is humid
enough. This was closer to the Gulf of Mexico, and to
use a term I picked up when we visited New York: *oy*.

A man came lumbering up to the car, a big man,
tall as well as overweight. He was wearing high-
heeled cowboy boots and one of those shirts with
Western trim. That, a ten-gallon hat, and a holster
with a big silver pistol in it. That and a lot of bullets
in a wide belt.

The badge on his shirt pocket said SHERIFF.

He walked right up to Jeet and said, "Son, your
headlights are still on."

Something in a far field glinted. I squinted, the better to see it, and was about to mention it to Jeet, but he was already in motion, harking to what the sheriff had said.

"Oh, thanks," Jeet responded over his shoulder, jumping back in and then staring at the instrument panel, obviously not remembering how he'd turned the headlights on in the first place.

"Rental car," I explained, briefly glancing at the sheriff and then looking back beyond him at whatever metallic thing had caught my eye.

The sheriff turned. "It's a car that you see over yonder," he said, pausing to spit on the cemetery soil. "It's got this here great big hood ornament on it. It's a big, fancy car, that's all."

But maybe it was the murderer, I thought. Don't murderers always return to the scene of the crime? I mean really, don't police sometimes videotape whoever's at the funeral for just that reason?

But the sheriff derailed my train of thought. "I know exactly who that is and why he's parked out there," he said, kind of puffing out his chest in a boastful fashion. The master detective at work or something.

Then his facial expression changed. "You a friend of the deceased?" he asked me.

"No," I said, "but my husband was." I gestured at Jeet, who was still inside the car and was now looking wholly exasperated. He'd begun flipping through the little instruction book that comes with rental vehicles.

The sheriff took a second or two to smirk. Then: "Sure was a shame about Towns," he said, shaking his big head. "Cut down in his prime. Looked like a tractor trailer hit him. He was plumb smooshed. I mean, head busted open like a pumpkin."

Towns had been the victim of a hit-and-run. Even

though I hadn't known him, the sheriff's description was vivid enough to make me catch my breath. "It was awful," I agreed. "Jeet and Towns grew up together," which was true, though they hadn't seen each other since they'd graduated from high school. Then Jeet had come to Austin and the University of Texas, where he'd met me, and Towns had gone to some little school in Georgia, where he'd met Della—or should I say Miss Macon, beauty queen.

"Any progress on the murder?" Jeet, his brow wet with sweat, had just rejoined us. Even though he'd been in the uncooled car a mere matter of minutes, there were big wet spots on his shirt and a tuft of his hair hung lank across his forehead.

"Murder?" the sheriff asked. "Don't know how it was that. In fact, a person might not have knowed he'd hit a man, I figure."

I looked at Jeet and saw him struggling with his composure.

The sheriff watched Jeet's face, too. He looked triumphant as he cleared his throat and spit snuff juice at Jeet's feet.

I knew it was snuff juice because he was holding a snuffbox in his hand.

"Yep," the sheriff said, really rubbing it in. "We put it down as an accident."

"Oh, right," I said sarcastically, and Jeet shot me one of those cautionary looks. The kind meant to shut me up.

Except that it was true. Granted, Towns had been out jogging in the predawn light, which is pretty much the only time you can jog in coastal Texas near summer without courting heat prostration, but still. You can't tell me you could hit a person and not realize it. I said exactly that.

"You could if your rig was big enough," the sheriff argued.

"Give me a break," I said.

Then Jeet tugged at me and gestured toward Della, who was standing next to the backhoe meant to cover Townsend up once he was in the ground. She looked small and depleted and I felt, I don't know, as if Jeet was right. This was an argument I shouldn't be having, especially not now. Because what mattered was that Towns was dead, not how it happened.

That and the upshot, which would be that we would be moving, bam, just like that, to Bead.

This wasn't just oy, it was double oy.

Except that all through the service, I found myself thinking how ridiculous this was, the notion that you could ream somebody on the street with your car or truck and just not realize it. I mean, you can run over a cardboard box and know it, feel the jar and the vibration jerk through your hands and up your arms. (Of course, it might be that this is the case only when driving my own truck, Mother, which is a '79 Dodge supercab with a host of idiosyncrasies. Maybe in normal vehicles, newer vehicles, these physical sensations aren't as pronounced.)

But in a podunk town like this, with a know-nothing sheriff, who could tell? People probably got away with murder every day in small towns like this. You know what I mean. Hunting accidents that weren't, or chemically induced heart attacks. The kinds of things you read about in true-crime books.

I looked around at the mourners, wondering if the murderer was among us. And suddenly I began to think murderers, plural. Because the cemetery looked to me as though everybody had been buried in it yesterday. I mean, at least a hundred fresh mounds of varying lengths and no grass at all. I mean, Forest Lawn, this wasn't.

And on the edge of it was a dilapidated old frame

building, kind of like the Gothic house behind the Bates Motel, sort of grayed by a century of indifference and harsh weather.

"Jeet," I whispered, but only got a resounding "Shhhh" in response. So I didn't get to share my *Psycho* analogy with him.

Instead I edged away, far enough to take a look at some of the tombstones. Forget being buried yesterday. These were ancient, with dates like 1804–1884, or 1816–1913. Not only were these old, but the people interred in them had lived long, long lives.

Go figure.

I looked up at the building again just as the sun disappeared behind a cloud. That was when I saw it, a face in one of the upstairs windows. It looked, I swear, just like the face of Anthony Perkins: lean, angular, homicidal.

I blinked, and the sun shot back out and, you guessed it, the face was gone.

I looked at the other mourners again, wondering if anyone else had seen it, but of course, all eyes— even the eyes of the sheriff—were on Della and the hole in the ground.

Accident.

I mean, think about it. For all anybody knew, Towns had been mowed down for writing some crusading article—maybe for trying to halt some big land development or discovering some big political cover-up. Couldn't the sheriff think about that for a minute or two?

Jeet probably had. In fact, if I knew my husband, he'd ransack the Bead newspaper morgue the first day he was on the job and pass whatever information he found there on to—who? The sheriff.

Unless he could bypass the sheriff and go right to the Texas Rangers or something. Except that Jeet wasn't likely to do that. He was much more law-abiding than I, more inclined to go through channels.

And anyway, on the way back into Bead, when I talked about Towns maybe campaigning against, I don't know, mob influence or something, Jeet scoffed and said he doubted there was any kind of hard news at all in *The Bead Weekly*. "Think about it," he said. "What could there be? It's probably all straw-berry festivals and good feeling." And even though he ought to have perked up at the mention of a food-stuff, he sounded momentarily disgusted at the sort of paper his chum had been putting out. He'd even punctuated the sentence with a derisive little snort.

Which was not like Jeet.

Apparently he and Towns had dreams of high-level journalism way back when. Still, Jeet seemed to be assessing his chum a little harder than he assessed everybody else. And it seemed especially weird since Towns was dead.

"You're probably right," I answered. "I can't imagine any land development here. Or even any politics."

"There are politics everywhere," Jeet said. "But you might be right about the land thing. God, did you see that building? Talk about a monstrosity. I'm surprised Towns didn't launch a campaign to tear it down."

That snort again.

"Probably because it's ready to *fall* down," I said.

And we both laughed.

Then we both looked around at the terrain in what was going to be our new home—a steaming-hot, mostly flat, sandy brown expanse with a tuft of wilted grass here and there—and stopped laughing.

Jeet squeezed me toward him. "You're a good sport, Robin," he said.

CHAPTER 2

The worst part about it was that Jeet had to start right away. Which probably doesn't jibe with the way most folks see a weekly newspaper in some podunk town like Bead working. What I mean is, people—even professional journalists—probably think it's an easy job.

Without boring you with a lot of detail—and this is mostly because I'm not sure of the detail—let me tell you: it isn't.

As a matter of fact, every single time I called Jeet—because by that time I was back at Primrose Farm getting our act together, so to speak—he sounded semihysterical. "Robin," he would shriek, "they are still pasting this thing up by hand," and I would try to make appropriate noises of sympathy, although I hadn't the vaguest idea what he was talking about. I kept imagining some Dickensian shop with everyone hunched over tall wooden desks and wearing those green eyeshades. And no, I don't know why.

The part I did get was that Jeet was not just editor, but editor and reporter and photographer and production crew, all four. There was someone who went around and sold ads, but apparently at a snail's pace. And like a snail, this ad person was seldom actually seen. Lack of advertising, according to

Jeet, was one reason that the newspaper was in such bad financial shape.

"How bad?" I asked. But the roar of the presses kicked off in the background and I didn't hear whatever it was Jeet had replied.

But I really didn't worry much, because once Della hired a replacement for Jeet, he and I would be out of there. I mean, it wasn't as though Jeet and Towns had been more than boyhood friends.

In fact, at Towns and Della's wedding, he and Towns had barely spoken at all. I remember puzzling about it back then, but Jeet had just brushed it off with a joke about Towns having other things on his mind.

On the phone, though, it occurred to me again, and I bellowed in order to ask Jeet about it.

He screamed, "What?"

"Remember the wedding?" I hollered.

"The what?"

"The . . . oh, never mind."

"The what?"

I hadn't really cared enough to keep shouting my questions out. And besides, Della was someone we weren't going to keep up with, probably, once this ordeal ended.

I know that sounds cruel and calculating, but listen, how would you be? I mean, I didn't know her from Adam and, after all, it was because of Della that I was right this minute pulling Plum and Spier into the blistering-hot and dusty parking lot of a feed store in Bead to ask if there was any place nearby where I might board them.

God, if horses could talk, they'd have probably been cursing. I mean, the trailer, which is normally navy blue, was a sort of reddish-tan color, that's how much dust. And I'm sure that the horses inside were coated in a shade that exactly matched.

And it had to be steaming hot back there. Even though dressage judges down here often sit inside horse trailers to stay out of the sun, there's usually a fan in there with them. My horses, poor babies, had no such luxury. I spent most of the drive alternating between grumpiness and guilt.

And on top of it all, it was June twenty-something, the summer solstice, which is the longest day of the year. That meant that the ridiculous heat would go on until way after nine that night. After nine-thirty, even. And it technically wasn't even summer yet!

So I was not in the best of moods when I entered the un-air-conditioned feed store. In fact, I had to talk myself into a facial expression vaguely resembling a smile. And usually I'm not like this. It was just that I felt so put upon, so turned upside down by this whole thing. And by whom? Not by a family member or a close friend, but by some total stranger, a woman who probably wouldn't recognize me if she ran into me on the street.

Plus—and this was no small matter—it was so incredibly stinking hot, hotter than usual. And I'd been dumb enough to wear jeans. I'd been out of the air-conditioned truck, what? Not even five minutes, and I'm telling you, if I'd have had to use the bathroom, I'd maybe have gotten the jeans down all right, but I never would have been able to pull them back up.

But of course, wearing shorts would have guaranteed what I call "fried thigh." That's when you get back into your truck and forget that the sun has raised the temperature of the upholstery to a skin-sizzling level in the scant seconds that you were off buying a diet Dr Pepper.

I'm ranting, I know.

Anyway, the clerk confirmed my view of the Bead

weather. "Lord," he said, "it's so hot, a person would have to die to feel any better."

I think ordinarily I would have laughed at such a folksy expression, but in this case, it was too true.

But also, at the mention of death, I couldn't keep my mind from zooming to the thought of Townsend Loving out there in the bare Bucking Hill ground.

Then I shivered despite the hundred-plus the mercury had hit. And it wasn't even lunchtime!

"Whew, yeah," I said, wiping the sweat off my upper lip with the back of my hand.

The clerk and I looked at each other. He didn't seem as though he was in a great mood either. We both tried to lift the corners of our mouths into something resembling a friendly greeting. Instead, I fear, we both looked mildly pained.

Well, I thought, why not go for it? "Are there any stables around here with dressage arenas?" I asked.

"With what?" The clerk's eyes were looking as though they'd sprung out on stalks.

"A place to ride," I rephrased. "Like with an arena or something." I had backpedaled somewhat, thinking, rodeo, cutting, roping, I didn't care. Actually, I'd have settled for just unloading the horses somewhere, like the side of the road, just to let them feel some air move over their bodies. Except that the feed store was right on the highway and Bead was, after all, the land of hit-and-run.

The clerk continued to look bewildered.

"Some level place, you know," I said. "A place without a bunch of cactus or mesquite or trees."

Talk about downsizing your dreams.

The clerk scratched his head all the same. "Arena," he repeated, staring at me all the while. As though the word would begin to take on meaning if he waited long enough.

Beyond him, scrutinizing the fly spray and salt licks, a small, youngish woman with hair cropped like a boy's seemed to be smirking sympathetically.

"Like, who buys a lot of horse feed here?" I asked, priding myself on my Sherlockian skills with that one.

"Don't know that that's any business of yours," the clerk said.

Over his shoulder, I saw the woman turn and look at me. Her mouth began to form a little O and her eyebrows shifted upward just a bit.

I lifted my own brows as a way of offering encouragement, a way of saying, "Yes?"

She even started walking toward me, I swear. I was sure she was about to rescue me, tell me she had a high-powered stable with a Grand Prix trainer and a covered arena with floor-to-ceiling mirrors just over the next hill. She took one step, then two. Yes! *I've been looking for someone to ride with,* she'd say. *You don't even have to pay me board.*

I was now actually smiling. I mean, beaming my broadest smile in her direction, when the clerk interrupted, stepping sideways into my line of sight.

The little fantasy I'd been having ground to a halt.

"Just who are you anyway?" the clerk asked.

"I am the wife of the new editor of *The Bead Weekly,*" I said, drawing myself into something that would, in terms of posture, mirror my newfound social status.

His demeanor changed immediately and his tone softened. "Oh, yeah?" he said, fishing into his pants pocket. "I've been meaning to put in a classified for this old pickup of mine," he said. "Would you mind taking it on in for me?"

I sighed and reached out for it, feeling more than a bit diminished. I looked around for the woman with the little-boy hair.

She had disappeared. Indeed, it was almost as if I'd imagined her.

"Who was that woman?" I asked the clerk.

"Don't rightly know her name," he said. "She comes in maybe once, twice a week."

"Isn't her name printed on her checks?" This wasn't any of my business either, but I figured that now that he knew who I was—or who Jeet was—he'd cough up the information.

"Don't use no checks," he said. "That one, she always pays cash."

"What does she buy?" I continued.

"Funny you should ask," he said, grinning for the first time. His teeth looked as though they'd been knocked out and put back in, one by one, most hurriedly. "Horse feed."

"She buys horse feed?" I repeated, as if making certain I'd gotten it right.

"Buys Athlete brand, too," he said. "Buys it a sack at a time. Puts it into a little bitty foreign car, too. I order it special for her, along with the feed that we mix up here."

Now I don't want to go into a discourse on horse feed and the relative nutritive elements of different brands. Suffice it to say that Athlete is pretty high-powered stuff. A backyard horse would probably be fed something with a little less fat and protein in it. Too much fat and protein would get a backyard horse overrevved. Plus a lot of it would be wasted. Athlete costs quite a bit. Maybe twice what standard feed does.

So this woman, you see, was probably a real find. I mean, maybe my alleged fantasy—the arena with the mirrors and all that—wasn't too wide of the mark at that.

"I've got to know who she is," I said, a little voice inside me whispering that this woman was a serious rider. Someone I could schmooze with. Ride with. Talk to.

The clerk shrugged. "Can't help you there," he said.

I looked at him hard. He's lying, I thought. I mean, Bead wasn't exactly a thriving metropolis. It was the kind of place where everyone would know everyone else. He had to know where this woman lived, right?

"Look," I said, appealing to his decency. "My horses are outside in the trailer. And it's broiling hot. Come on."

The man brightened. "I got a cousin who's fixing himself up a real nice place for horses. Close in, too. It's on Garner Street."

"A pasture? For horses? Your cousin?"

"Yup."

Did this seem weird or what?

"Is it fenced?" I asked.

"Yup."

"With barbed wire?" I asked, almost sure that it would be yup again. And there was no way I would place my precious babies in a field that was fenced with the perilous tendon-tearing, hide-ripping stuff.

"Nope," he said. "Goat wire. Like over yonder." He pointed at a roll of perfectly acceptable woven wire on the floor near the door.

"Does this place have water?" I asked. I felt my eyes narrow. There had to be a catch.

"There's a spigot and a hose that runs to the trough," he said. Then he cocked his head and looked at me suspiciously. As if wondering why I seemed to be going out of my way to rule out his cousin's place.

And he was right. For some perverse reason, I was doing that. Maybe because I didn't want to relinquish the indoor arena and attendant amenities that I'd conjured up earlier in conjunction with the woman I'd seen.

Not that the realization of this made me—a person who'd been ready to settle for air moving over her horses' bodies a few minutes ago, right?—stop. "And is there a shelter?" I asked.

"There's a great big shed." He spread his hands apart to indicate its mammoth size. "He's even bought himself some hay he could maybe let you have. Maybe even for nothing," he said. "Like, he was asking me about hauling that hay off."

This was too good to be true. Had I forgotten something I'd done that day? Like, sold my soul to the devil, maybe?

But apparently not. Because the next thing the clerk said was, "There's just one thing."

"Yes?"

"My cousin?"

"Yes?"

"He's mean."

"Wait a minute," I interrupted. "You mean he doesn't like animals?"

"Oh, naw," he said. "Booger, he likes animals just fine. It's people he don't much care for."

"Oh," I said, unduly relieved. "No problem. I can deal with that, I think."

I could deal with it because I know a lot of people who are exactly this way. Sometimes, in fact, I'm that way myself. I mean, think about it. Animals are so simple. So direct. They never have a hidden agenda. Animals are so easy to satisfy, so easy to please.

People, on the other hand, are always saying things they don't mean, doing things they'd rather not, or not doing things they want to do.

People are a mess. So who, with a brain, wouldn't prefer animals to people? Generically, I mean.

Or maybe I was just crabby enough about being in Bead to empathize with Booger's point of view.

"How long has Booger been around horses?" I demanded. I told you, I wasn't in the best of moods.

"Oh, he's always had him a horse or two, seems like," the clerk said. "Had him a spotted horse—gelding—not so long back."

"Had? You mean he doesn't have him anymore?"

"Nope. Horse died."

Aha! "Died? Of what?" All of the hideous possibilities began to run through my mind, neglect chief among them.

"Old age, I reckon. Gelding lived, gosh, must be twenty-odd years. I used to pet that thing when I was just a kid. Booger wouldn't never let me ride him, though. He was mean, like I said. Even way back then." The clerk's voice took on a petulance that meant he was still, after all these years, holding a grudge.

"Just how do I get to Booger's place?" I asked.

I walked out to the parking lot with a little lighter stride. Though I'd opened the little doors at the front of the trailer, neither Plum nor Spier was looking out. I don't blame you, I thought as I made my way toward the rig.

Jeez. What was I letting them—letting myself—in for?

As I neared I saw someone by the rear of the trailer, as though about to open the back doors to unload. Except that the person slipped away very quickly, before I could really see who it had been.

My general impression, though, was of a man—rather bony, too. But there wasn't any vehicle nearby. Just a field with tall, slightly withered weeds.

But none of the weeds was moving, the way they would have been had a person entered there to hide.

I wasn't alarmed by the notion of someone having

been there. People are always drawn to horses. They always want to pet them or give them treats. They always want to ask you questions about them. So the presence of someone at the back of the trailer wouldn't be exactly strange.

Moving away like that at my approach, that's what made me uneasy.

But as I've already established when recounting my encounter with the feed-store clerk, I was sort of looking for trouble. Looking for stuff to gripe about, at least.

And anyway, the feeling of uneasiness was fleeting. Less than fifteen minutes later I was tooling Mother down a residential side street. There were little white houses, bungalows, and trim little lawns.

No kidding, it was what, in the 1950s, must have been the suburban dream. Now, in the 1990s, the scrawny saplings the early inhabitants had planted were big pecans and elms that arched toward each other over the narrow street. This was a city neighborhood now. At least as close to city as you could get in Bead.

And it wasn't unattractive, either.

It was straight out of early television sitcoms, the kinds of houses where the kids said, "Gosh, Mom," and "Golly, Pop." Where women were housewives who wore aprons and men were office workers who wore suits.

Which was great except for one thing: it didn't look like the sort of place where I was going to find a stable. The clerk at that feed store, I decided, was the one who was mean. He'd led me astray, knowing what I'd have to go through to turn a truck and trailer around on narrow streets like these.

Except that just when I was thinking this, I saw it: the little house at the end of the street and the adjoining pasture-cum-shed.

"Glory be," I said out loud.

Because it was a kind of model setup. About an acre surrounded by a woven wire fence and a nice, seemingly dry shed, and what appeared to be a lockable storage area next to it for hay and maybe even tack.

What was more, the ground beside it looked as though it had been scraped clean and leveled. Almost as though the man had known I was coming and thought, This woman will need an arena.

And, on top of that, it was cross-fenced, so that I could keep one horse locked up on one side of the field while riding the other horse on the other.

So my problems were solved. Or almost, anyway.

Because the only other thing I had to do now was get the misanthropic Booger to like me.

Which I think he did until I got to the part where I was telling him about the uncanny way that Plum and Spier can tell time.

"I feed them in the morning and again at three o'clock every day, see?" I said, flashing my biggest smile and probably—I mean, I was that disgustingly interested in installing my horses there—batting my eyelashes, too. "And if I'm more than five minutes late"—flash, flash, bat, bat, giggle, giggle—"they just carry on like crazy. I mean, Plum bangs on the water trough with her front feet and Spier uses his—"

"Say what?" he interrupted.

"Plum bangs with her . . ." I was smiling and carrying on, still not getting it.

"On that metal trough out there?" Booger asked, no smile in return.

My own dwindled. "Well," I hedged, "not really hard."

"Hard enough to hear?"

My voice was more like a squeak. "Well, uh . . ."
Great.

The moment was tense. He'd already agreed to a price—fifty dollars a month; I'd buy my own feed and he'd sell me twenty bales of coastal Bermuda hay at an unheard of dollar per; and I'd pay any amount more than his usual water bill. Indeed, he seemed—well, not happy, but somehow okay with the idea of supplementing his income this way.

I stood there thinking: Me and my big mouth about the banging on the trough. And meanwhile, time—and my heart—stood still. I mean, Plum and Spier were still in the horse trailer, hot as blazes. Not that I hadn't offered them water to drink. It was just that it had been a long, long trip, and while I'd been inside the truck in air-conditioned splendor, they'd been back there being horses.

Baking, I mean.

If they kicked against the metal sides of the trailer, it would be over then and there, I knew. I tried to beam them a message: *Please be still.*

And they were, more or less. Oh, you could see the trailer move a little as one or the other of them shifted weight. You could hear a slight metallic sound whenever one or the other of them moved. But basically, they were being wonderful horses.

Booger glanced at me and then at the trailer and then back at me. He expelled a stream of air that made his lower lip shake.

This man, I thought as I waited for his response, could put Alfred Hitchcock to shame in the suspense department.

Oh, please, I secretly begged. Openly begging was going to be next.

"What kind of riding you say you do?"

"Dressage," I said.

"Dressage," he repeated.

"Right. Dressage." I wanted to add, *But I could switch. What kind of riding would you like me to do?*

"Well, missy," he said at last, "you got yourself a deal. But you listen to me. If those horses wake me up one time, I'll be sending you down the road with them. Because I need my sleep."

Phew. I was in.

"I'll be here at seven A.M. sharp. And three P.M., too," I began blathering. "I promise. They'll never bang on the trough, never. And if they do, I mean, if they even look as though they're going to, I'll . . ." What? Tie little inner tubes around their feet. Something, anything.

"I don't care about the morning," Booger said. "I work the night shift, see? So in the morning, they can bang away to beat the band. But if there's any banging going on out there at three o'clock in the afternoon, you'll just have to take them horses someplace else."

I raised my hand, Girl Scout style—or was it the Pledge of Allegiance? I can't remember. I raised my hand as if testifying in a court of law. "I will never be late for the afternoon feeding," I said. "I will be here at three P.M. on the nose every single day. I swear it."

He squinted at me, as if measuring my trustworthiness.

"All right," he said at last, folding my check and tucking it into a back pocket.

"By the way," I asked, "who boarded here before I did?" I just couldn't believe he'd done all that he had to the place for a twenty-odd-year-old gelding.

"Boarded?" he asked.

"Who kept their horse here?" I kept on. "Was it

maybe some kind of youngish woman with short black hair? Kind of looks like a boy?" I made scissor-like motions in the direction of my own chin-length brown bob.

I figured I'd try her because his place looked serious enough for someone buying Athlete to ride in. And also, because she was local and maybe he knew her.

He cocked his head and looked at me. The gesture was very much like his cousin's, back at the feed store. Except that Booger's face turned bright pink and his voice seemed to shake.

"Do you know this woman?" he asked.

"No. I saw her in the feed store. I just thought she might be, you know, someone you maybe knew or someone I could ride with."

"You fixing to bring her here?"

"Huh?"

"I said, are you fixing to bring this woman with the short hair here to ride these horses with you?" he repeated, at a new and higher decibel level.

His voice still quavered, though.

His skin tone had deepened. He was magenta now. A very becoming shade, actually. I figured he didn't hate her or anything, he just didn't want anyone who wasn't boarding there riding on his property. Liability or something. "No, hey, don't worry," I assured him.

I watched him take several deep breaths. As he breathed he returned to his more or less natural shade of beige. I thought I'd better engage him in more conversation, though, just to make sure he was past the danger point. I mean in medical terms. Because he had sure looked to me as though he was about to have a stroke or a seizure or something. God, did I remember CPR?

And anyway, what was the big deal? Did he spend his Sunday evenings watching *60 Minutes*? I decided to put his mind at ease. "I think your regular homeowner's policy would cover someone getting hurt," I offered.

His eyes narrowed. It was almost as though they wanted to merge into a single eye in the space above his nose. Oh, God, I thought. He thinks I'm the suing type. But I didn't say anything about that because it was not the moment to be discussing lawsuits, even if my point in mentioning them was going to be that I would never ever file one or bring one or whatever the correct terminology is.

Except that, in truth, he did not appear to know what I was talking about.

Even I was almost not sure.

"So . . ." I tried another, simpler tack. I mean, maybe the woman in question was just someone Booger hated. "Do you know her?" I went on. "The woman with the short black hair?"

I was treated to another color change, a purpling yet again, accompanied by one of those long, suspense-creating looks. And then finally he spoke. "I don't know nothing," he said, his voice an angry whisper.

Sheesh.

I guess you're thinking that I shouldn't have boarded the horses with a guy like this, a guy who blew hot and cold and whose own cousin said he was mean. A guy who got apoplectic at the thought of some nonpaying person riding on his property, but listen: It had been a long dusty trip and the place was really nice, and I don't mean just for Bead.

It was tidy and it looked safe, and there was hay here that I could use, so I didn't have to go off in search of any. Furthermore, the guy already had my check.

I smiled, sort of, gave a little wave, and went on about my business.

I opened the little doors up by the horses' heads and undid their ties. They were both sopping wet, as though they'd been out galloping. But of course, sometimes, here in Texas, in the heat, horses get that way just standing around under trees.

So I canned the sympathy and went on with the unloading procedure. "You're home, guys," I said.

The thought of Bead as home made me feel a little hollowed out inside. But I had to press on, for Jeet's sake, at least.

I opened the back of the trailer on Spier's side first. It distracted me from my self-pitying frame of mind. Because unloading has become, now that I have two horses instead of one, a real follow-the-rules procedure.

I've learned the hard way to let Spier come off the trailer first. Which is to say that he pitched a royal fit the one and only time I unloaded Plum before him.

I'm not kidding. We are talking major hysteria here. My trailer still bears dents from his protest. People get huffy. Horses get hoofy. He was hoofy up one side of the thing and down the next.

But Spier isn't a naughty horse. He just got it into his head that he was being abandoned and—well, he did what any of us would do if we were being left in the lurch.

Think of Dylan Thomas and "Do not go gentle . . ."

Plum is just the opposite. She flat out doesn't care. Or else, to put it in a positive light, she couldn't conceive of anyone leaving her.

Plus she gets to chow down some more, yanking for a little while longer on the hay net that I keep in the trailer if she stays behind. She's insouciant, very sure of herself and of me.

Anyway, I unloaded Spier and tied him, then did the same with Plum. They both looked around as much as their ties would allow. They were excited, sort of dancing a little, so that it would have been hard to get their leg and tail wraps off right then.

So rather than bark orders at them, I waited. Then, when they were still enough, I started unwinding.

I didn't bother rolling the wraps right then, but left them in little heaps on the ground. Blue heaps where Spier's had come off, and red ones for Plum.

Then I took them—again, Spier first—in through the nearest pasture gate so they could explore their new digs.

And they had a blast, trotting along the fence line as though to test it, snorting and occasionally shying. Then something scared Spier and he took off, leaping and bucking, his tail standing out like a stick.

Soon he and Plum were racing around together. I'd think—Oh, no!—because they'd look as though they planned to leap the fence for sure and take off for parts unknown. But then, at the last minute, they'd skid to a halt.

I'd just relax again when, boom, they'd be off full-tilt again, back legs flying upward, huge farts tearing the air.

I love horses. Love watching them careen around this way. I almost wished that someone—even Booger—had been there to share the moment with me.

Except that the minute the thought of him

crossed my mind I figured, Whoa. What if all this
bucking and running amok would worry Booger, because after all, the horses were kind of divoting up
the pasture as they ran. You could see little clumps
of it being launched into the air. Still, I knew they'd
quiet down soon enough.

I swiveled toward the house, wondering for a moment if I ought to stop there and say something re-
assuring. Like offer to reseed after I move out or
something.

There he was, in the doorway, watching the
horses' hijinks. Maybe it was the light, but I
thought I could see tears glistening in his eyes.

Maybe he was thinking of his gelding.

But anyway, isn't it really something the way
horses can win people over? I mean, they'd have to
be able to do that, just in order to survive. But still,
horses can thaw the coldest heart.

I turned away so that Booger wouldn't know I'd
seen him that way.

Except that it was too late. He'd seen me. Oh, well.
We'd have a sentimental bonding moment, I thought.
He'd tell me what a kind horse his gelding had been
and I'd smile appreciatively as he reminisced.

"Hey," he said, "you there."

"Robin," I said brightly. "You can call me that."

He wagged a finger at me. "Don't you go thinking I've got a soft spot," he said. "Don't you go
thinking these horses can be making noise and
carrying on late in the day."

So much for the meltdown.

"They won't," I said. "I promise." But at that very
moment I was even sorry that I'd told him to call me
by my first name.

CHAPTER 3

The newspaper was in a little metal building—kind of like an indoor riding arena only a lot smaller. The building sat smack in the center of a concrete lot. I could drive all around the building, which pleased me more than I ought to admit.

I was pleased because, in addition to driving Mother, I was still pulling my extra-long, extra-wide, extra-tall two-horse trailer, sans inhabitants, of course.

If you've ever tried to back a horse trailer of any size, you'll understand my elation at the drive-around part. It isn't that the task can't be done, and even by me. It's just that if there's any way to avoid having to do it, I do.

Mother doesn't have power steering, for one thing, and there is no deodorant in the world that can't be overpowered by my backing efforts. (I actually think that backing a trailer is a universally loathed thing, because our dressage club has a trailer-backing contest as a fund-raiser every year and it is always a whopping success. One year a TV crew came out and ran some footage of the event on its sportscast.)

But anyway, you're probably wondering why I was tooling around Bead with an empty horse trailer, right? Why hadn't I left it there at Booger's, where Plum and Spier were walking around and looking for things to squeal and kick up their heels at?

The answer is that I hadn't been able to get up the nerve to ask Booger if I could leave the trailer next to the pasture. I hadn't wanted to press my luck.

So there I was, tooling around outside the newspaper office with my enormous blue, dust-disguised albatross in tow.

I pulled to a stop beside a long window through which I could see Jeet. He didn't even look up, though I don't see how my rig couldn't have registered at least on the periphery of his vision.

But his vision was fully trained on whatever it was on the stack in front of him. An enormous stack of papers and envelopes. A stack that had to have been accumulating for years.

I sat there with a kind of sappy smile on my face watching him as he worked. He did look mildly anguished, but I'd seen that look before. Usually when he was trying to write, groping for the perfect word, the perfect word order.

Jeet is like that, very language-oriented. If he isn't reading the *Larousse Gastronomique*, he is curling up with Sir Thomas Browne or Edward Gibbon. I can't tell you how many of my intimate in-bed moments with my husband have begun in the presence of a volume of *The History of the Decline and Fall of the Roman Empire*. It's not a power thing he's reading, though. It's usually the menu of some emperor's culinary debauch. No kidding, I probably ought to write to Dr. Ruth about it.

But anyway, it had been ten whole days since I'd seen Jeet or talked to him, really. Oh, yes, we'd called each other on the telephone, but there wasn't a phone in the place he'd found to rent. "Why spend the bucks for a month?" he'd said, commenting on the hundred-dollar-plus installation fee that Southwestern Bell charged to put a phone in. "We can always talk when I'm at the paper."

The latter, about talking while he was at work, hadn't proved to be possible. For one thing, he was always harried. For another, over the sound of the heavy machinery that I guessed were the printing presses, we both had to scream. Even then, it seemed like everything had to be repeated at least two or three times.

Our exchanges were wholly unromantic, things like:

Me: I miss you.

Him: What?

Me (louder): I miss you.

Him: You what?

Me: Never mind.

Him: What?

He had written me a single letter. From his handwriting, I'd say he'd dashed it off. It wasn't a love letter, at least not to me. It was a love letter to the food that he was having to do without. Olive oil, the kind that comes in a gilt-trimmed bottle, and really grainy mustard, and Oregon herb bread and sourdough and French-roast coffee. Oh, and food accoutrements, like his garlic press and his coffee grinder.

Which is not to say that looking in through the window at him, I didn't feel a kind of teenage gooshiness. This was heightened by the knowledge that Jeet was doing a heroic thing, filling in for his dead friend Towns.

So now that I'd installed the horses happily somewhere, I wanted to collapse in my husband's embrace, right? I mean, who wouldn't? (And in exactly that order, which the horse owners among us will definitely understand. The others will write nasty letters about how put-upon poor Jeet is and how maybe they could do better. At least they'd like to try.)

I shut Mother's engine off and ran my finger

through my bangs, thus preparing myself for emergence into the heat.

Despite all the time I'd spent in the parking lot musing, Jeet still hadn't even looked up. He was deep in the middle of something, a little vee in between his eyes indicating his concentration. His hair was standing up in one spot like one of the Little Rascals—Alfalfa, I think. That meant he'd been raking his hair with his hand, which in turn meant he was calling his fiercest focusing powers into play.

Maybe I shouldn't go in right now, I thought.

Except that once I'd exited Mother's cab, the hot, moist air was like an assault. I had to get inside the building or I'd die.

Die.

Oh, God. The whole reason we were here.

It made me wonder about Della. Was she at home moping around the way I'd have done if our situations had been reversed? Or was she, as the saying goes, keeping busy? Keeping her mind off the fact that her husband had been mowed down on the street.

Had Jeet talked the sheriff into making any progress on that?

I headed inside, hoping fervently that, even as antiquated as Jeet said the paper was, the place would at least have some big, freestanding fan that I could stand in front of.

I couldn't have been more wrong.

The place was air-conditioned. Air-conditioned! Oh, how lucky can a person be?

If this were a perfume commercial, Jeet would have looked up, his features would have softened, and he would have swept me into his arms and given me a long, fervent kiss.

As it was, he lifted his gaze and said, "Oh my God,

no. Is it Tuesday already?" He grabbed his calendar, tore off a couple of pages, and crumpled them. "I thought you were coming tomorrow. Oh, jeez, Robin, I'm nowhere near done."

I was more than a little stung. Feeling my face going red, I said, "Well, jeez yourself." Snappy rejoinders—in a crunch situation like this one—are not my forte. My remark was accompanied with something that I suppose resembled a pout.

Jeet's expression changed and he reached out for me, catching my hand and jumping up to enfold me all in one gesture. "Oh, gosh, Robin, I'm sorry. I'm sorry," and he swayed with me for as long as it took for my petulance to subside.

"I really am glad you're here," he said. "It's just that"—he lowered his voice and whispered—"I'm so overwhelmed here. You just wouldn't believe."

"Why are you whispering?" I asked, keeping my voice as low as his.

"Because Della's in there." He pointed at a partition. "I don't want to hurt her feelings."

Just then a roar so huge began that I swear I jumped into the air. If I had been holding something, I'd have dropped it, convinced that I'd somehow been moved to a runway at JFK or something.

Jeet laughed at my reaction. "I know," he said. "That's what I did the first time I heard it, except that I was holding a cup of coffee at the time."

It was the roar that all along I'd thought was the printing presses, except it seemed to be coming from one of the ceiling vents.

"It's the throbbing heart of the universe," Jeet shouted.

"The what?"

"The air conditioner," he said at the top of his

lungs. "It's probably the oldest one in the state. It belongs in the Smithsonian."

"Where?"

"The Smithsonian."

"Where?" I asked again.

"Come on." He began leading me back toward the door. "Let's get some lunch."

But I was laughing. Because the whole thing about not being able to hear reminded me about the last time I'd gone to lunch with my mother.

My mother, the soul of decorum.

There we were, in this fancy little place, with white tablecloths and gleaming crystal and starched-looking waiters hovering around.

My mother was talking about running into an old friend of hers. "She's so easy to be around," my mother was saying. "Minutes after we'd run into each other, there she was, talking about . . ." She looked around and lowered her voice and whispered something.

I thought I heard the word "china," but I wasn't sure. "Her what?" I asked.

My mother said it louder.

"Her trip to China?" I asked, closer, I thought, to figuring it out.

And the next thing I knew, my mother was bellowing, "Her dry vagina," in a voice so loud that people walking by on the sidewalk could have heard.

The only equivalent restaurant story happened when I had lunch with a breeder who had been expecting a shipment of frozen semen for days and who kept yelling about how, if she didn't get her semen "that very day," she was going to be very very mad.

"Maybe you could do a feature on racy restaurant stories," I told Jeet once we were outside the building.

"Huh?" he said, distracted.

*   *   *

And then we were in Jeet's car, heading out toward the highway. "We'll go to Smokers," he said.

"Smokers? It isn't a barbecue place, is it?" Jeet knew my feelings about that, but there might not be any choice. I could do beans, I thought, and potato salad, maybe. Which is not to say that I'm a vegetarian. I eat some meat, but it has to be ground up and not look as though it's part of an animal. It's a weird thing, I know, but it's the way I am.

"No," Jeet said. "It's . . . oh, well, you'll see. You can get eggs or grilled cheese or something."

He had that frown again.

"What's wrong?" I asked him. I still hadn't been to wherever it was we were living, although Jeet had told me on the phone it was, and I quote, "more than adequate," a little furnished house that one of the paper's advertisers owned.

He pulled to the roadside and parked, engine still running. "Everything's wrong," he said. "Oh, God. I'm up to my eyeballs, and the paper had about forty typos in it last week that I didn't catch, and stuff kept falling off the page because I hadn't stuck it on tight enough, and I have to go out and take pictures at—oh, I don't know, the Wal-Mart that's about thirty miles from here in Darren, and I'm so tired, and Robin, nothing ever happens here. Nothing. I don't know what to write about, because nothing ever . . ."

This wasn't like my husband. It was more like me.

And his lament continued, ". . . and you can't get anything here, and . . . You did bring that stuff I asked for, didn't you?"

I nodded yes. Yes to the coffee and the olive oil that I told you he'd asked for. That, and the garlic press, etcetera.

". . . And the sheriff hasn't been to the paper once, so I think they've written Towns's whole death off," he continued, "and besides . . ."

I waited with my breath kind of on hold. Because, I don't know if you've ever noticed, but when people are giving lists of reasons for things, the *real* reason, the important reason, always follows the phrase "and besides." Listen next time and see.

Jeet said, ". . . I missed you so much every night that I thought I'd die."

Even though we've been married forever, my heart went zing. I scooted toward him as much and as fast as you can scoot in a bucket seat and we kissed like honeymooners for a couple of minutes.

Because I knew what he meant. I mean, sleeping with Jeet—the actual sleeping part—is totally wonderful, the press of his skin against my skin, even if we're lying back-to-back. Or the way he'd casually drape an arm or a leg over mine. I'd been missing it, too, missing it like crazy, and it made me wonder more than once what Della must be going through. But anyway, Jeet finished kissing me and continued with his food rant.

"I ordered a patty melt at the Dairy Queen," he was saying. "A simple patty melt. And guess what?"

I couldn't.

"It came on white bread," he said. "White bread." He sat back and waited for my response.

"Boy," I said noncommittally.

And fortunately he explained. "Rye bread. A patty melt has got to be on rye. I just couldn't believe that they could call something on white bread a patty melt and get away with it."

I tsked sympathetically. Jeet was probably picturing a lynch mob.

"And one time, at that place we just passed, I

ordered popcorn shrimp. Robin, they were like little erasers. The size, the texture. Like those little erasers that they stick on pencils. At least at Smokers," he went on, "they know how to poach an egg."

"Ah," I said.

"And there's a guy in there who can make a tolerable omelette, too," he went on. "Of course, you have to go there at . . ." He paused to look at his watch and said, "Jeez. We have to eat fast and get back. I'm supposed to take pictures at the something-or-other insurance company. They just put in hanging files or something and Della says I should—"

"Hanging files?" I asked. "That's a picture?"

He sighed deeply and pulled back onto the highway. "Yes," he shrilled. "In Bead, that's a *front-page* picture. Can you imagine, Robin? I'm not joking. That's a front-page picture. Some woman in a beehive hairdo standing in front of an open file drawer with a great big grin on her face."

I could see that he'd been waiting for the opportunity to complain about all this and I was glad that the hearer of the complaint had been me. I mean, the guys I'd met so far in Bead might not be attuned to woes like these, know what I mean? Oh, the newspaper stuff, maybe, but the patty-melt thing? Never. They'd have assumed that Jeet wore women's underwear underneath his khakis or something. And God forbid they should find out he was a home ec major! There'd be no living it down.

It's just temporary, I reminded myself. But imagine if it weren't! "How did Towns ever do it?" I asked. He'd been in Bead for five or six years before his death. Maybe his brain had died years before.

"Beats me," Jeet said.

And then he started telling me about the letters to the editor.

"They read like *Finnegans Wake*," he said. "There's one woman who's always making testy references to the Bolshevik Revolution. I can't, for the life of me, figure out what she's trying to say."

"Do you print them?"

"Of course." He threw up his hands. "How else would we fill the pages of this rag? I'm telling you, you can forget the notion of some investigative piece getting Towns killed. It's just one triviality after another. I mean, just the other day . . ." And he was off and running again, this time talking about a feature called "Yard of the Week." "I not only have to interview the people who live there about their portulacas and their petunias," Jeet was saying, "but I have to take pictures of their yard. You can imagine it. Plastic swans and Lucite birdbaths and—"

"Little jockey boys with lanterns," I finished. "God," I said. "How many years has that been going on? I mean, that's fifty-two yards a year. How can they keep finding nice ones?" Especially since I hadn't seen any. Yards that should be photographed, that is. Next thing you know, Jeet would be reduced to photographing that old house out by the cemetery. Ha! With a tombstone garden, I thought, smiling at my own joke. "So how do you avoid duplicating yards?" I asked.

"What?"

"You know. How do you keep from picking yards that have already been done? Like, well, do you look at the back issues of the newspaper, or what?"

Jeet looked guilty. "I've been meaning to," he said. "But right now Della pretty much tells me what to cover. I'm getting so that I can predict it, though."

"Like . . ." I began, expecting him to fill in the blank.

"Like when a guy with a Ford dealership approached me about doing a feature called 'Truck of the Month,' I told him no." He shrugged.

"Yeah, I don't see Della as someone who'd be into trucks." As I spoke I pictured her as she was that day in the cemetery. "How's she holding up?" I asked.

He rolled his eyes. "Maybe it's a facet of the grieving process, I don't know," he said, "but she's in here at the crack of dawn, and she stays long after I leave. She just locks herself in Towns's office doing God knows what."

"Has she interviewed anybody for the editor's job?" I asked him.

He pulled into a gravel parking lot filled with pickup trucks. Some were in worse shape than Mother. "Not that I'm aware of," he said.

Great.

The sign read SMOKERS W, which rang some sort of bell.

"You're thinking of the 'Trespassers W' sign in *Winnie the Pooh*," Jeet said, "and from what I hear, the place started out in just about that way."

Except I wasn't thinking about *Winnie the Pooh*. Maybe I should have been, but I wasn't. I was thinking about something that was almost within my mind's reach. Almost. You know how crazy making that can be.

Smokers W.

Smokers W.

I kept repeating it to myself while Jeet blabbed on.

"It was the owner's protest against all the anti-smoking regulations," Jeet was saying. "He had his name up there. It was Chester or something and a huge 'Smokers Welcome' sign. Then a big wind came along and whooshed away all but what you see."

"And he never replaced it?"

"I guess not. In fact, I heard he took it as a sign from God or something."

"A sign to do what?"

"I don't remember. Whatever it was, it seemed pretty farfetched to me. You know how these stories go."

"What stories?"

We were inside now, and the air, as you might imagine, was thick with cigarette smoke. And the place wasn't air-conditioned either. It had the big standing fan that I'd imagined finding at the newspaper office, and it was kind of moving the shafts of thick gray fumes this way and that.

I looked at Jeet, amazed at just how far he'd be willing to go for a decent poached egg. Pretty far, I guessed, since he had probably never in his life held a cigarette between his lips.

"You'll get used to it," he told me, reading my mind. "Believe me, it's better than the swill they serve at the other available choices."

My gourmet husband, forced to eat swill!

"Actually," he corrected himself, "that statement wasn't entirely fair. The chef who—"

"This the missus?" A small, quaky, birdlike man interrupted.

"Indeed." Jeet's voice was tinged with pride. "Robin," he said, "I'd like you to meet Tooter Brown. Tooter's our ad salesman."

Ad salesman! It looked as though he'd need a good wind to cross the street. I could see his—well, I'm not sure what bones they are, but those two nobby ones just where your neck attaches to your torso? Are they collarbones? Anyway, I could see those poking through his shirt.

"Sell anything today?" Jeet asked.

Wrong question. Tooter dropped his gaze and muttered something about how he had to be moving on. Then he shuffled through the smoke and toward the door.

Jeet and I looked at each other across the table.

"My God," I said.

Jeet shrugged. I could see that he liked Tooter and didn't want to say anything bad about him, so I let it drop.

Then we segued into typical travel talk. He asked how my trip had been and where I had the horses ensconced. I regaled him with the story of my encounter with Booger. When I told him where the pasture was, he said, "I'll be damned."

"What?"

"That's a couple of blocks away from the place I rented. No kidding, Robin, you could walk there."

I reached across the cigarette-scarred Formica surface and took his hand. "Whew," I said. "Things are coming together after all."

Something flickered across his face. "Are they," he said, his voice flat with discouragement.

"Whatever it is, we can get through it," I told him, wishing that I felt the certainty that my voice conveyed.

I know, you're thinking I'm a hypocrite or something, but I'm really not. I'm just a horse person. A horse person develops a way of saying "Easy," or some other there-there kind of soothing word even when terrified. Because to let that terror be known is, when dealing with horses, a major mistake. It merely escalates their own.

So I was horsing Jeet into feeling better, all the while I was thinking *Yuck* about Bead in general and *Yikes!* about the fact that whoever had run

Towns over was still somewhere in the universe driving around.

I looked at my fellow diners.

Every single one of them looked like a possible murderer to me.

The only woman in the place was the waitress, and she looked like someone who had been a wrestler in the not-too-distant past. Her face was sort of marbled like hamburger meat and her eyes were dead. Needless to say, she did not smile when she took our order.

Well, my order. She seemed to know what Jeet was going to have.

The only good news was that they didn't have diet anything. I ordered a classic Coke. Then I had to have a hamburger and fries, because what else would you have with a Coke?

This couldn't go on. At this rate, I would probably balloon up to a hundred and eighty pounds by morning and be unable to get into even my Lycra riding breeches, I thought.

In fact, everyone in the place, except for Jeet, was beefy and huge. And looking at their plates—heaped with chicken-fried steaks and mashed potatoes and thick white gravy—I could see why.

Then the door swung open and a new prospective diner walked in.

He was as thin as Jeet.

He was the Anthony Perkins look-alike. The one I thought I'd imagined seeing at the funeral.

CHAPTER 4

We were about to turn into the newspaper lot when Jeet suddenly braked and, simultaneously, groaned, "Oh, no! Oh, blast. I guess it's too late." And then, after this sudden jerk, he accelerated and continued toward the building, the look on his face turning into one of grim resignation.

Near the entrance along the side—the one from which Jeet and I had emerged—was a dapper gray-haired gent in crisp white pants and a Hawaiian shirt that, on a younger person, would have been considered quite trendy.

"What's the matter?" I asked Jeet.

"That's Boone DeWitt. He's always had some burning desire to be a reporter, apparently, and now that he's retired, he's hoping to indulge it. No kidding. He's always after me to do some story or other and Della says he's crazy as a loon."

"What kind of story?"

"Who knows?" Jeet said. "It's all I can do to stay out of his way so that I don't find out."

"But maybe he'd be good," I said. "I mean, you say you're overwhelmed and here's this guy—"

"Robin," he interrupted. "Look at him. He's a hundred years old. What kind of story could he do?"

I looked. He was maybe sixty-five. I mean, there

are dressage folks—coaches and riders both—who are in their seventies and still really fabulous.

I said this, but Jeet was not convinced. He was arranging a smile on his face as DeWitt approached.

"But you say you're swamped," I went on. "Plus, you're being an ageist."

Jeet spoke under his breath. "The point is, Robin, the whole town is full of people just like Boone DeWitt. He's not the only one. If somebody gets a new bull or puts up some preserves or some pickles or if someone—I don't know—rearranges the living-room furniture, they think it's worth a story, and if they can't write it, they want me to."

Although Jeet is always correcting even my most minute grammatical lapses, I did not feel that now was the time to mention that his pronoun (someone) and antecedent (they) did not agree. I had a better idea. "Maybe I can help you," I said. "I could write some stories. Then you wouldn't have all that work to do, and I could meet some people and—"

Jeet looked at me skeptically. "What kind of stories?" he said, interrupting me.

"Like about horses. Like, there's this woman with real short black hair that I met at the feed store, and she buys really high-protein feed, so she must have performance horses of some kind—"

Jeet wouldn't let me finish. His eyes got that glazed-over look that they get when he's protecting himself from excessive horse talk. "Robin," he said, "no one here is interested in horses. Of all the things they've approached me about covering, horses was not one of them."

"Well, I could do other stuff," I said, a wee sullen note creeping into my voice.

"And it's 'whom,' not 'that,' " Jeet said.

"Huh?"

"A woman *whom* I met, not a woman *that*—"

But I was saved by the tapping on the driver's-side window that DeWitt had undertaken.

Jeet took a long, deep sigh and turned the engine—and thus the air-conditioning in the car—off. He saved us from suffocation, however, by rolling the window down. A cloud of hot, sticky air moved in at once. I could feel my hair going limp and my skin getting damp.

DeWitt hunched over, wide-eyed. He smelled of some sort of flowery cologne. I kept wondering how he kept bees from following him. "Got to talk to you, Jeet," he said, dropping an age-freckled hand over Jeet's forearm. There was a note of urgency in his voice. "Someplace private. No fooling, boy. This is big."

Jeet looked down at the man's hand and then up at his face and then turned to look a little quizzically at me.

"Really big," DeWitt said.

He seemed sincere to me.

"Let's go inside," Jeet told DeWitt. And then he gestured at me. "And this is my wife, Robin. She can come, too."

The man looked at me warily. "I don't know," he said.

Well.

That certainly piqued my interest.

Now I was *dying* to hear. Particularly since Jeet had apparently decided to take the man seriously for once. Unless, of course, faced with a decision between a story by me and a story by DeWitt, Jeet had chosen the latter.

Unless—and this could be it—something about DeWitt's demeanor made this occasion different from others in the past.

The old gent eyeballed me and evidently decided I

was okay. Either that or else the sweltering heat had swayed him. In any case, he didn't protest as the three of us trooped through the side door into the disheveled offices of *The Bead Weekly*.

The outer door closed behind us to reveal the throbbing heart of the universe in full swing. Deafening though that made things, it was a blessed relief to go from the oppressive midday heat to utterly cool within seconds.

Which means my mother was crazy when I was growing up, always telling me that going from hot to cold to hot would make me sick. If that were the case, everyone in Texas and probably Oklahoma, too, would be sick all the time. I mean, think about it. We're always having to run through the outdoor oven to get from one air-conditioned spot to the next. The only alternative would be to become a total recluse, but an air-conditioned recluse.

"You're not going to believe this," DeWitt hollered over the air conditioner, thus interrupting my private rant. "I've found a witch."

"What?" Jeet shouted back.

"A witch," DeWitt hollered again.

"What?" Jeet called.

"A witch," I screamed, having somehow, perhaps because I was slightly left of the vent instead of directly in front of it as Jeet was, heard.

"A witch," DeWitt boomed again, just as the air conditioner shut itself off. So the word just filled the now too silent room. It seemed to hang there in the air.

And as if conjured, Della, still dressed in black, was standing there in the corridor, a stack of newspapers cradled in her arms like a baby.

We all three rushed toward her, apologizing. I'm

not sure why, except that was our mode. Maybe we were afraid she'd think we'd been talking about her.

She ignored what we were saying, though. She gave me a hello that would have been perfunctory under any circumstances, but which, given that I'd just arrived from out of town after a ten-day interval between now and her husband's funeral, was downright odd. It was a sort of twist of her head, almost a dismissal.

Then: "Jeet," she said, as if I didn't exist. "We have to talk." And with that she turned on her heel and headed back to what had been Towns's office.

I guess you can forgive the newly bereaved just about anything.

"Sure," Jeet said, pecking my forehead, shaking DeWitt's hand, and following her.

Which left me standing there with a man I'd been led to believe was certifiable.

"So," I said, absentmindedly picking up a long, narrow reporter's notepad and a pen that had been lying near it.

This comforted DeWitt, I could tell. He took a deep breath and began to talk slowly and with apparent thought.

"I was out scouting that area across the river just about dawn."

"Scouting?" I asked.

"For birds," he said. "I'm a birder. Among other things, of course."

"Birds," I repeated, and wrote that down.

"Look. As crazy as it sounds, there was a witch out there, setting things up for some kind of service or something."

Do you know the theme music from *The Twilight Zone*? Hum it right here.

But I didn't do that. I nodded sympathetically

and scribbled, exactly the way I'd seen Jeet do over the years. I didn't look up because I was afraid I'd give away what I was thinking—that this guy was crackers.

Except that Jeet had taken Boone DeWitt seriously.

So maybe I ought to pay better attention and not be so quick to judge.

"It's some kind of cult," DeWitt said. "I wrote down the name." He dug in his pocket. "I could take you out there and you could see for yourself. I know it sounds insane, but it was so very strange, I don't see what else it could be." He handed me a scrap of paper.

Twilight Zone reprise.

In fact, I had to fight to keep from humming it out loud now.

Because on the paper was one word, a name. *Kehmbe.*

I thought about making a smart-aleck remark, like, *Oh, sure, the goddess Kehmbe. She demands that an adult male virgin be sacrificed every full moon. Of course, there's a problem finding an adult male virgin,* or some such. I mean, this man was gone.

Or else there was an enclave of Ashanti somewhere over the hill.

I mean, there are a million explanations, none of them rational.

"I don't know," I said, trying to hedge. "I just got into town and—"

"I told you," he said, "it sounds crazy, but there she was, plain as day, this witch, setting out this here name in a field. I watched her through my binoculars doing it. She carried out this here *K* and then this here *E*, and then—"

"What? They were separate letters?"

"On concrete blocks. They were painted just as big and plain as could be, one letter on every block."

I looked at the word again.

Kehmbe.

Could it be?

Of course. It wasn't a name, it wasn't a word, it was a series of letters. And they were letters that I knew. The curious letters that, all over the world, are used to surround the small dressage arena.

I closed the notebook and looked toward the door behind which Jeet and Della were safely closeted. No point interrupting them, right?

"Okay," I said, "take me there." Because I knew what this had to mean. I had found the black-haired woman I had seen at the feed store, right? The one who was buying the high-protein feed.

"You want to go right now?" DeWitt asked, as though even he couldn't believe that I was willing to trundle on out there with him.

"Sure," I said. "Why not?" It was, what? Maybe one-fifteen in the afternoon at the very latest. I could still get back in time to feed. "It isn't far, is it?"

"Nope." He rattled his car keys.

And so, without even leaving a note for Jeet, there I was, following a triumphant DeWitt outside into the blazing cusp-of-summer heat.

CHAPTER 5

Most of you already know that, although the word "dressage" literally means training, dressage, these days, is a competitive equestrian sport—an Olympic sport, no less. And some of you know that it calls for a rider to enter a rectangular arena and perform different movements at different places. Places that are marked by letters of the alphabet along the perimeter of the arena. (There are also imaginary letters down the center line, but I won't go into that right now, okay? Because this is just a quickie explanation.)

To really simplify things here, a dressage test will say something like:

At K walk. At B trot. So the rider will walk when his knee passes the letter *K* and trot when his knee hits the letter *B*, okay? I mean, that's a total simplification, but it gets the point across.

The letters are important, because precision in dressage is important. I can remember painting the letters on coffee cans that Lola and I stuck out in a field so that she and I could practice doing things the way we'd have to in shows.

Really, I always imagine that traces of the letters will be found on those huge stones at Stonehenge or that astronauts will sight them on the surface of some distant planet.

But nobody knows exactly how the letters that are placed around the periphery of the dressage arena were chosen. At least no one I have ever asked. I mean why they aren't *ABCDEF* instead of *KEHMBF*.

(And yes, the last letter is *F*, not *E* as in the goddess Kehmbe, but I figured that was a legitimate mistake for DeWitt to make. I mean, he thought he was witnessing some arcane witch ritual. His hands were probably trembling, right? And Kehmbe at least sounds like it could be a name. An odd name, sure, but a name. On the other hand, Kehmbf makes no sense whatsoever.)

Don't write me letters about *K* not being the first letter. I know many people would say the letters begin at the letter *A*, where all tests tell the rider to enter. Just use your head, though:

If you ride in at A, and you're in the regulation small arena, the letters will be arranged around you on the rectangle just the way DeWitt had written them: KEH along your left side, a C in the middle opposite the A, and MBF down the side opposite.

DeWitt, or the person he thought was a witch, had skipped the C.

Lola taught me how to remember the order, a sentence that read like a *National Enquirer* headline: KILLER ENZYMES HARM CRAZY MISS BANKS'S FACE.

But then there's the regulation *large* arena, which adds a few letters in between. Lola had a way to remember this one, too, which went: KILLER VICIOUS ENZYMES SERIOUSLY HARM CRAZY MR. RAOUL BANKS'S PRECIOUS FACE.

I once went to a recognized show where the people who set up the arena had gotten two of the letters out of order. The organizers thought I was crazy as I tried to explain. "It's Killer *Vicious* Enzymes," I kept saying, as though Lo and I had adopted a universal mnemonic rather than a personal one. "You have Killer *Precious* Enzymes."

Finally the technical delegate, the person the American Horse Shows Association insists a show have on hand to settle such disputes, strolled over. She was, thank God, someone I knew. "Robin Vaughan is right," the delegate told these people, who seemed about to have me removed to what is politely termed "a structured setting." Except that the delegate explained things a little more clearly and rationally. "You have the P where the V ought to be," she said. And things calmed right down and the show got under way with God in his heaven and all things right with the world.

But the point was, the witches' coven that Boone DeWitt had stumbled upon was anything but. It was the refuge of a hard-core dressage rider, and as I mentioned, I'd bet anything that she had short, boy-cropped black hair.

"You been a reporter long?" DeWitt asked me.

"Oh," I said, "not so very."

He stopped and looked suspicious. "What exactly have you covered?"

I said, and not untruthfully, "Well, an international smuggling ring, for one thing." But then reality took a brief hold. "Of course, my husband is the real journalist in the family," I said.

DeWitt smiled wistfully and started walking again. "Two journalists working side by side," he said admiringly. "What I wouldn't give . . ."

Well, Jeet and I had never actually worked side by side. Unless you count the number of times I've accompanied him to restaurants he was reviewing. I'd say things like, "Too salty," or "Mmmmm," which I guess counts as some sort of contribution. Other than that, I was kind of exaggerating. Maybe even lying. I mean, I had done the international smuggling story I'd alluded to, but I'd sort of blundered into it. But maybe you already know that. Anyway, I felt a little uncomfortable, basking in glory that I hadn't earned. Still, I wasn't going to tell him and blow my chance to see the dressage arena.

"I'd be a great journalist," he said. "I really have a nose for a story."

"I'm sure," I said.

"I know that husband of yours doesn't think so, but it's true. I read all the tabloids," he said.

"Well!" I tried to sound upbeat and positive. But now I kind of understood why he'd leaped to the witchcraft conclusion.

"My copter's on the fritz," he said, indicating a highly civilized version of an overland vehicle, the kind with the tire strapped onto the hood that you see going out on safari in PBS specials. His was white and, like his trousers, spectacularly clean. No kidding, even the aforementioned tire.

"Cool," I told him, hoping fervently that it was. Just the little jaunt through the newspaper parking lot had rendered me hot and sticky again.

But I shouldn't have worried. Boone DeWitt's Jeep was outfitted with everything but a hot tub. No kidding: there was a phone, a television set, and even a little bar in there.

"I guess your husband told you I'm a businessman," he said, as if that explained the opulence.

"What business?" I asked.

"Oh, oil, of course. After all, honey, this *is* Texas."

"Hmmm," I answered. A far cry from newspapering, too. Or, for that matter, writing books about the foods you've grown up with. "I thought oil went bust," I said. "I thought oilmen were hurting."

He looked stunned. "But I *am* hurting," he said.

"Why do you think we're in this Jeep instead of up in my helicopter? It's going to cost a cool ten thou to get that puppy up in the air again. June and I have been cutting back like mad. Why, when winter comes, we aren't even going to heat the pool except when we're getting ready to use it."

Imagine!

Still, some perverse instinct made me want to top him. "Jeet didn't even get a phone," I said. "Because the installation fee that Southwestern Bell makes you pay is so high."

"Why get a phone?" DeWitt countered. "He can always call and talk to you from the newspaper."

I said, "Yeah, well," thinking about the huge rumbling that was the a/c. Then thinking about how utterly chintzy rich people can be.

"And," he said accusingly, "didn't I hear that you have horses?"

Horses. Right. Own a horse and—in the eyes of the world at large—you're automatically rich. Never mind how you struggle to keep them in oats and hay and shoes. Never mind.

I couldn't even muster a response. I just sighed deeply, knowingly.

"Ha!" he said, his face lighting up. "Gotcha on that one."

I debated whether or not to tell him that I'd bought my last dress-up outfit at Second Looks. Then I figured that instead I'd better go back to the task at hand. Let him think that I burned a hundred-dollar bill every morning just to light my way to the barn. What did I care? "This witch," I said, "did she have short black hair?"

Before he could answer, my body listed sharply to the right. Boone DeWitt was swooping around some other driver on the road.

"Holy cow," I said.

"What's the matter?" he shouted. "Can't take a little adventure?"

Adventure, right.

"Listen, DeWitt," I tried. "Why are you in Bead?"

"I live here," he said.

"I know that. What I mean is, why? How long have you been here?"

"Twenty-two years," he said.

"And why Bead?"

He screeched to a halt right there in the roadway and turned his entire upper body toward me. The look on his face said he thought I was a total dope. Nonetheless, he explained. "Because the place is oil rich. It makes the Permian Basin look poor. Hell, it makes Kuwait look—" He'd stopped talking. His eyes were on his rearview mirror.

"What is it?" I asked.

"One of those double-wides coming down the road," he said, starting forward. "I'm not sure there's room for them to get around us."

I turned and shrieked as I saw a home, an actual home, about to ram the back of DeWitt's vehicle.

But I shouldn't have worried. DeWitt shot ahead with, oh, heck, nanoseconds to spare.

And to think that I'm afraid of riding a horse over jumps!

DeWitt looked over at me and laughed. "You'll get used to it," he said.

"I'm not sure I want to," I told him. My God. The thought of him piloting a helicopter!

He checked his mirror again. "Guess that mobile home is the start of it," he said.

"The start of what?"

"Oh, a big trailer park out by the river. Pretty controversial."

"In what way?"

"Oh, the environment. There's some kind of toad out there that environmental groups say ought to be protected."

"Wow," I said. "Jeet could write about that."

"Been done," DeWitt told me.

"By . . . ?"

"Townsend Loving," DeWitt said. "The man churned out a ton of copy about the project."

"Where?"

"Right here. In *The Bead Weekly*."

I sat and pondered this. "You mean," I said at last, "that Towns defied, say, some rich developer? And that maybe that's why Towns was murdered?"

"Murdered! Where'd you ever get that idea?" he said.

"He was mowed down," I protested.

"Hit-and-run," DeWitt insisted. "An accident. And anyway, the whole thing was defused. They found a whole bunch of those toads at some state park in Bastrop. So the whole environmental brouhaha went up in smoke. Happened long before Towns died."

"Oh."

I fell into a funk. I mean, here was a story big enough to have been a motive for murder, except that it was old news.

Still, I was reluctant to let it go. "Did Towns have any enemies?" I asked.

Boone DeWitt got the strangest expression on his face. A look that was knowing and ironic, too. "He had one," he said. "One enemy in particular."

"And that would be . . . ?"

"Not now," he said. "There it is." He was pointing at a driveway on the right. We flew past it, but not before I'd had a chance to note that it was long and deeply rutted. "Why aren't we—" I meant to ask why we weren't turning up that road, but he seemed to read my mind.

"When you're dealing with witches," he said. "you've got to go off-road."

Off-road. The man drove suicidally *on*-road and now we were going *off*? Oy. And to think that Jeet wouldn't have a clue about where to find me. Or, as it were, my remains.

"Look, DeWitt, I . . ." I was about to try to talk him out of the off-road thing when he looked in his rearview again and blanched.

"Oh, no," he said. "Duck."

"Duck?"

"Get down," he said, reaching for my head and swerving across both lanes in the process.

Jeez, I thought. Maybe DeWitt had run Towns down. And I was willing to accept the sheriff's theory, too, about how it could have happened without the driver realizing it. This driver, anyway.

"Stay down," he said. "It's my wife." He hauled on the wheel and made first a U-turn, then a stop.

I stayed down while he powered the window open. "Hi, honeybunch," he said.

Honeybunch had the voice of a Valkyrie. "Boone DeWitt," she said. "Are you out chasing some hare-brained story again?"

"Who?" he asked. "Me?"

"Boone DeWitt," she said. "You were sent out to buy some birdseed. Now see to it that you do just that and then get yourself back home."

"I'm on my way, Junebug," he said cheerfully.

I didn't hear her reply. Only the threatening tone of her voice.

Then the window whooshed back up and we started, once more, to roll.

Now he began talking to me under his breath, his

lips clamped together. Kind of the way a bad ventriloquist might.

Which I guess made me the dummy.

"She's right behind us," he said through his teeth. "When we get back, I'll park and lead Junie away. You wait a few minutes. Then, when the coast is clear, make your getaway."

"What do you mean, my getaway? Why can't you let her see me?"

"Who?"

"Your wife?"

"Uh-uh," he said. "It wouldn't do for her to see me with you."

Well. It was flattering, in a way. "What? Is she jealous or what?" I asked. Or was he in the running for the Senator Packwood award or something?

"Oh, it's nothing like that," he said. "She's bound to find out you're the editor's wife. Then she'll put two and two together and know I've been hanging around the newspaper again. You heard what she thought right off. That I was out chasing a story."

"You're a grown man," I said. "Why can't you hang around the newspaper? What could she possibly object to about that?" I asked. My back was starting to ache. Plus I felt stupid, all hunched over, half on the floor, and carrying on a conversation with a guy who wasn't moving his lips.

"Nope," he said. "Junie gets plumb upset. I told you, didn't I? She thinks I ought to be out earning more and more money."

Right. Gotta get that copter in the air. Gotta heat that pool. But no, he hadn't told me. "Money isn't everything," I said.

"Ha!" he said, ignoring my remark. Which he probably wouldn't have agreed with anyway.

His lips were moving again. "She's pulling off.
Gonna make a hairdresser appointment, probably.
So we're home free."

Except that I need a chiropractor, I thought,
creaking myself upright.

"We could try again tomorrow," he said.

"I, uh . . ."

"Tomorrow then." He pulled to a stop and almost
shoved me out into the parking lot at the paper.
Then he roared away.

I went inside to tell Jeet about the story possibilities I'd come across. The oil thing. The new trailer
park. Maybe even a toad update. Except that Jeet
and Della were still closeted inside her office.

With my ear pressed against the door, I could
hear as much. Della pontificating. Jeet uttering an
occasional, "I see," and "Uh-huh."

Then the throbbing heart of the universe kicked
in and I gave it up.

I sat at Jeet's desk, looking out the window at the
long, dust-covered expanse that comprised Mother
and my horse trailer.

It wasn't even two yet, and I didn't have a
thing to do until three, when it was time to feed.
Why wait here? I asked myself. I knew where to go
now, so why not drive out to the witches' coven on
my own?

I'd get to meet the black-haired woman, and seeing my trailer and all, she'd know I was a fellow
horse person. She might even remember having
seen my rig and me at the feed store. And when I
told her about DeWitt and what he had thought
about the letters, she would toss her head back and
laugh and laugh and laugh.

We'd laugh together. It would be instant bonhomie.

CHAPTER 6

I drove around the building that housed *The Bead Weekly* to avoid, once again, the necessity of turning the rig around. Except that then I managed to turn to the left rather than to the right.

Small matter. I took the easy way out again and, rather than back up, decided to traverse an entire city block.

Well, I'm making it sound bigger than it is. I mean, I was still in Bead, and it wasn't exactly like going around the block in Detroit or New York City or even Austin.

But the decision to do this put me in a whole new part of town. Which was fine, since Bead was going to be my interim new home.

Might as well see what the rest of the place looks like, I thought.

It was an older part than any I'd seen before.

And it was just like going back in time.

There, for instance, was the downtown drugstore, its big marble soda fountain visible through the window. There were people sitting on the swivel stools. People actually wearing bobby socks and saddle shoes!

This was unbelievable.

And more unbelievable still were the cars parked diagonally in front.

Old cars. Fifties, probably. A boxy Ford, for instance, and an old Mercury, both kind of drooping behind, probably from the weight of their fender skirts.

One of them actually had fuzzy dice hanging from the rearview mirror.

It was irresistible.

The witch, I decided, could wait for a fifteen-minute soda break at least.

I pulled Mother across to the other, more empty side of the street and parked, straddling sideways, a space meant to park eight cars diagonally. But hey. When you're pulling a two-horse trailer, what are you supposed to do? And anyway, there was another car parked there in the same illegal way, some fancy-schmancy job, a Rolls, I think, that took up three of the diagonal marks in the same sideways fashion that I had.

If a Rolls could do it, I could do it, I reasoned.

I hadn't seen what June DeWitt had been driving when she'd overtaken her husband, Boone. Since they were so rich, maybe it was she who owned the Rolls. Judging from the voice, I should look for an aging Amazon, Birgit Nilsson in her sixties or something.

I crossed to the soda shop and wandered inside.

It was a popular place.

In addition to the fountain, there were big wooden booths along the back, and they were filled with people of all ages. They all looked healthy and glowing, very rosy-cheeked. Corn-fed, you'd have to say, although the word very probably occurred to me because I was in this teeny-tiny town and not a big city.

And retro dressing was definitely in.

Or else it had never gone out.

God. Men were even wearing those slouch-brim hats!

In the center were little round tables with bent-wire chairs. They were filled with folks, too.

There was a high-school-age couple at one of them sipping an old-fashioned soda together—you know, the same soda, with each of them sucking on a straw.

The only thing bad about the place was the lighting. God, was it ever bright. I had to blink several times, and still it didn't seem as though my eyes would adjust.

I was about to slide onto one of the elevated stools in front of the long marble counter when I noticed one of the people sitting there.

It was Tony Perkins again!

But hey. I know everyone has got a double somewhere. This was clearly Perkins's double, the person I'd been seeing around town. Because even I know that the real Tony Perkins—the one who did *Psycho* and *Psycho II*—is dead.

I felt suddenly emboldened and walked toward him, about to speak. But a voice bellowed out before I could. "What the hell is she doing here?" it asked.

I looked around, still blinking, and saw that everyone was staring at me.

And everyone included . . . except no, it couldn't be. But it sure did look like Clint Eastwood on one of the stools, and Kevin Costner off in one of the booths.

Sure, I told myself.

"Hey, Bobby," someone hollered, and Clint turned around and asked, "What?" So it wasn't Eastwood after all. "Jimbo," the someone continued, and Costner answered to that. So okay, these were look-alikes, but still. "We'll have to do a retake," the voice said.

A tall man with a ponytail came striding over. "Who the hell are you?" he asked.

"I'm Robin Vaughan," I said, answering his question. He looked familiar, too.

"Do you have any idea what a retake is going to cost us?" he asked.

So okay. Disembowel me, already. Like I knew they were taking pictures or something. "No," I said, "I don't."

"I ought to make you pay for it," the man said, his eyes bearing down on me like searchlights.

I tried to make light of it, hoping that would cheer him up or at least make him stop looking at me that way. Sheesh. "I wouldn't be able to pay," I told him. "I don't have any money. And my husband is the editor of the newspaper here, so he doesn't have any money either."

"What did you say your name was?" the ponytail asked. He didn't seem at all cheered, either.

"I'm Robin Vaughan," I said, kind of huffy myself now. I mean, I'd gone out of my way to be friendly.

"Oh, is that so," the man said. "Well, you can tell your husband, Jeet, for me that we're grateful for the coverage."

"Oh, well, you're welcome," I said, puzzled because the man sounded angry rather than grateful.

"That's sarcasm, hon," the man said. "Della would have done a whole issue on this production, but not your guy. No. Your guy blows the whole publicity department off. The truth is, I'm having your guy fired. It's probably happening right now, as we speak."

"Oh, right," I said. If Della fired Jeet, just where would she be?

"Get out," he said. "Get out before I have you tossed."

That got my back up. I mean, I wasn't going and that was that. Just who did this turkey think he was. "I want a soda," I said, kind of disappointed to hear my voice sound like a whine.

But who cared how it sounded. I could hear the kids who were sharing the soda slurping at the bottom of theirs and it really got my taste buds activated. Plus I was taking a stand.

"I want a soda," I repeated. "And I don't have to go anywhere that I don't want to go." Even I could tell that I sounded about nine years old.

The man ignored that part of things. "I want you gone," he said. "Now, either you go on your own steam or I'll have someone throw you out."

I thought, Oooh, the story I would get Jeet to write about this! I had never been treated that way in my life. I would get Jeet to slam this drugstore up one side of *The Bead Weekly* and down the other. Or else I would. I'd write a letter to the editor. I might even contact *Texas Monthly*. I mean, really. Who did this guy think he was?

But now two shirtless bald guys—kind of cute shirtless bald guys, actually—came to stand behind the ponytailed man who was doing the talking.

"What's going on here?" I asked. I was starting to get scared. Like, maybe they were going to turn ugly, like a lynch mob or something. I mean, there's that side of small-town life, too.

All three men looked at me with suddenly big, suddenly wide eyes. Then they looked at each other. I've seen that look before, a kind of can-you-believe sharing look that other people sometimes exchange in my presence.

So I don't know everything, okay. But anyway, they decided to cut me some slack.

"We're making a movie," the one who had seemed familiar—the tall one with long hair—said. "Do you mind?"

A movie.

Suddenly the clutter in the background came into my field of vision, crystal clear. The lights, so many of them, and so very bright. The wires, miles and miles all looped and coiled. And the big metal trunks, all with SMOKERS W emblazoned on their sides.

Smokers W.

That was why I hadn't thought about Winnie the Pooh in that restaurant. Because Smokers W was a Hollywood production company, a two-bit one, to be sure, but one that had gotten a lot of publicity because of the movies it made.

Christian vampire movies.

Vampire movies where the would-be victim holds up a cross, and instead of recoiling, the way vampires normally do, these vampires fall to their knees and convert.

All the movies were exactly the same. Only the settings changed. There had been a cowboy-and-Indian one, and an upper-crust British one, and now, obviously, there would be a small-town America one.

"Look." I tried to recover. "I know you. You're . . ." But his name—he was the director and the head of Smokers W combined—wouldn't come to me.

"Alfred Hitchcock," the man said, stepping aside to address his goons. "Get her lost," he instructed them.

The guys grabbed me, one on the left, one on the right, and lifted my feet off the ground. And it came to me then, the man's name. He was Kat Karston.

Of course.

And it could have been worse. I mean, at least his movies were fun, in a campy, over-the-top kind of way. They were a lot better than those big, soft-focus nostalgic movies, the kind where nothing much happens but they're so slow, everyone thinks they must be especially subtle art. I've never actually seen one all the way through because I kind of doze off, but they get really good, kind of smarmy reviews and you know that if you ever say out loud how bored you are, people will think your education ended in ninth grade.

Anyway, that was him, Kat Karston, I realized as the bald men lifted me off the ground and deposited me, feet flailing, upright in the street.

Jeez. I would talk to Jeet. In addition to a rant about the way these people had treated me, there should obviously be something in the paper about them being here at all. I mean, a movie! Jeet clearly hadn't realized what was going on when he'd said no to the publicity department. He probably thought they were just trying to get him to cover one more small-town thing.

Except that the movie people obviously knew Della—I mean, Karston had even mentioned her by name, which probably meant that Towns had given Karston's movies a lot of coverage in the past.

In the past!

It meant that other movies had been made in Bead.

God. That meant that it could really have been Clint and Kevin in there. Except that another of Kat Karston's trademarks was that he used celebrity look-alikes all the time. Couldn't afford the real thing.

In the upper-crust English one, for instance, the vampire had been played by a ringer for Lady Di.

Jeez. I'd had a brush with fame.

When I told people back home about it, I'd leave out the part about being thrown out.

*　　*　　*

I got into Mother and revved up the a/c. It was ten past two, which meant the heat was approaching full force. Still, I thought as I glanced at my watch, I could still make it out to the edge of town to meet the black-haired dressage rider and get back in time to feed Plum and Spier.

Heck. Maybe I could even bring her back with me when I fed. Except thinking that reminded me instantly of Booger's reaction to my mere mention of her.

So I'd meet her and run, maybe set up a time to come back and really schmooze.

I pulled forward, cruising past the feed store on my way out of town.

The clerk was out there coiling a garden hose in the parking lot. I honked at him—just to be friendly—and he looked up at me and frowned.

Ah, Bead.

I was tooling along on the road that DeWitt and I had traversed earlier. It passed, I noted, the little cutoff that led to the cemetery. The one Jeet and I had traveled in procession behind the hearse.

Not that I wanted to be reminded of that.

Except that there was another procession in progress, and it didn't look like a funeral.

The cars had placards all over them, but I only made out what one of them said:

GRAVE ROBBER.

I rolled the window down and heard a lot of honking and shouting. One of the words bandied about seemed to be "ghoul."

Another movie, maybe?

I didn't want to get mixed up in that.

And besides, if I started down that road, I wouldn't be able to turn around without backing. I sure didn't want that.

Plus it wouldn't get me any closer to my goal,

which was to meet a kindred soul, a fellow rider, the
owner of a dressage arena.

There it was, the rutted drive I'd seen.

I braked slowly and evenly, from habit, and crept
into the turn.

This, of course, comes from hauling horses
around, babying them through corners and stops.
Because it's very hard for them to keep their bal-
ance back there, even if they do have four legs.

The driveway was a real challenge, even though
Mother is set up pretty high. I wondered how the
woman's little foreign car—I was thinking Lamborghini here—could make it without bottoming
out. I wondered, too, if she didn't maybe have dogs.

Big Rottweilers who would come barreling out to
greet my unannounced visit.

Or, like my friend Marilee, rest her soul, a brace
of vicious little Chihuahuas.

But only silence greeted me.

Silence and an air of despair.

Because, oh, God, was it ever a run-down little
place. You know the kind I mean. Littered with
rusted-out abandoned junk.

Like the carcass of a Toyota. Only its tires
seemed to be intact. Every surface was pitted. It
even had bullet holes in one of the doors. As if
someone had tried to put it out of its misery.

And a rusted-out travel trailer, too.

It was up on concrete blocks, sort of listing to the
right.

Except that it wasn't abandoned at all. Because
as I neared it I could hear, unmistakably, the steady
whir of an air conditioner!

*   *   *

Still, I couldn't imagine a horse out on this wasted land, much less a dressage horse who ate Athlete.

Of course, there was still no guarantee that the person who worshiped the goddess Kehmbe was the same woman.

Surely DeWitt was mistaken about the driveway or something. I'd come to the wrong place.

Except that as I moved away from the trailer and the noise that the air conditioner made, I heard it:

Hoofbeats.

The unmistakable half-a-league, half-a-league three-beat of the canter.

I started up over the rise toward the sound.

CHAPTER 7

Although I hadn't recognized her in the feed store, it took only a few moments of actually watching her on a horse to pin down who she was.

Tiny Rochambeau.

She was an extremely effective rider, but a little deficient in the grace department.

I know, who am I to talk?

Except that you know what I mean. Some riders are like dancers, very liquid, very lithe. Tiny wasn't like that. Except that she got wonderful stuff out of her horses anyway, and right off the bat, without wheedling or nagging. That's what I mean by effective. She didn't have to ask a horse twice.

Not that I'd ever seen her ride in person. I'd watched her on tape. She'd made bunches of tapes.

I know you're wondering why, I mean, if she wasn't the world's greatest rider. Well, the reason is, she was a wonderful teacher. No kidding, she could explain things, demystify them, the way no one else seemed able to.

And that makes sense. I mean, the way she talked about this skill on the first tape in her series was that she had had to struggle with riding herself, and therefore she knew what to do to overcome bad habits or crappy position. Natural riders, natural athletes, she said, just did whatever it was they did, and ofttimes couldn't explain it. It was too intuitive.

Anyway, Tiny Rochambeau had made a fortune, I assumed, making these videos. And I used to see her name in magazines, too, advertising her availability for clinics. God, Lola and I used to fantasize about taking clinics with her.

Then, all of a sudden, she stopped. I mean, you didn't see her name anymore.

But there she was, out there on Coronado, the horse she used in the tapes, and there he was, cantering a ten-meter circle as easily as he would have one that was forty.

That's the thing about great dressage: it's so difficult, what the horses are doing, and yet looks so effortless.

But why was Tiny Rochambeau here, on this woebegone piece of property in the woebegone little town of Bead?

I decided I'd hide out, watch for a bit, and then, when Tiny looked as though she'd finished working the horse, I'd stand up and ask her exactly that.

Do a story on it for Jeet, too, I thought. I mean, even he had to be impressed that a rider of Tiny's renown had taken up residence here.

I stayed as low as I could, but the horse evidently sensed I was there. He had been coming across the diagonal—and yes, there they were in the little makeshift arena that Boone DeWitt had thought was some sort of witch's sacrificial ground—changing leads every second stride. But Coronado—probably because he knew I was hiding out there—kept blowing it.

"What's the matter, big guy?" I heard Tiny ask. "Let's try it again, what do you say?"

And she'd patiently do just that. After another

misfire, to which she responded just as understandingly, he did it just fine.

And she didn't push him to do ones, either. She pulled him up after he'd done his twos correctly and then she patted him. "Good show," she told him, and I could hear the sound of her hand against his neck and the grateful little snort he gave in response.

I was impressed. A lot of riders would have started whomping on the horse, insisting that he perform. Tiny could tell that something was wrong and worked her horse through it. And now, I figured, might be the time to tell her—albeit apologetically—that the something that had been wrong was me.

Tiny was unusual in a lot of ways. She taught jumping for one thing. In addition to dressage, I mean. And I remember hearing that she actually jumped her horse—I mean took him out on the trail and popped him over brush and coops and things. This is really rare with a horse so far along in dressage. You tend to baby a horse more as he gets up there, as if you didn't dare risk a wreck and thereby lose all that training. A lot of dressage horses are only ridden in arenas and see open country when they're turned out, period. *If* they're turned out.

This doubled my admiration for Tiny—that she'd let her horse be a horse.

I stood up to approach her.

Coronado had been facing pretty much the opposite direction.

Even so, he reacted to my sudden appearance—because horses, with their eyes set far on the sides of their faces, can see all around them—by bolting.

I really hadn't thought he'd do that. I mean, here was a horse who had been around the block a few times. Still, there was no denying that I'd spooked him.

And worse, for a minute it looked as though Tiny was going to come off. I mean, Coronado's sudden shot forward hurled her pretty thoroughly backward and it looked as though she would go flying off, maybe even somersaulting, right over his rump.

Instead, she just got left behind, but seriously enough so that her legs left the horse's sides and went up in the air for a minute like some Thelwell cartoon.

The biggest sin, though, was that she jerked backward on the reins.

I felt awful.

But then, somehow, she managed to stay on board and even pull herself upright. It still took a good bit of distance before she managed to slow Coronado down. And by the time she did, he'd galloped to the tree line on the far side of the field.

She didn't blame him, though.

In fact, I could hear her laughing as she got him to slow down to a walk and then a halt. She stood there for a few moments in silence and then she moved off and disappeared into the woods.

Probably cooling him down, I reasoned.

I really envied the matter-of-fact way she'd dealt with what could have been a total disaster. I mean, me, I'd beat myself up over it. Especially the jerking-back-on-the-reins part.

She just thought, Whoops, I nearly lost that one, and went on.

You see that in shows all the time.

Mediocre riders, ordinary riders, make one mistake and that's it. They blow the whole rest of the ride.

The really great ones mess up and just shrug it off and go on.

But anyway, while she was cooling him off, I figured I'd have some time to reconnoiter.

Considering what my hiding had done, I thought,

too, that maybe I'd pretend to have just arrived. Because, even though she'd been cool about everything, I didn't exactly want to admit that I was responsible (a) for Coronado blowing his changes and (b) for her almost falling off because I'd made him bolt.

I dusted myself off and began walking along a path of sorts. A place that was more worn than the ground around it.

Sure enough, I came to an enclosure that was probably the horse's stall.

It was touching, in that it was constructed of what seemed randomly gathered scraps of things. Boards were different widths and clearly different ages. The tin that was used for the shed was old, kind of hammered and bent, with a lot of surface rust and even some old nail holes. But it was safe looking and snug looking despite the materials.

Still, I felt a little weird that there I was, at Booger's, in surroundings that, compared with these, were paradisal.

And why did Booger have such a wonderful place anyway?

Why didn't Tiny?

I mean, Tiny was an actual dressage person, a serious rider, and here she was, using the equivalent of the local dump. Meanwhile Booger, who had probably never been on anything but a backyard horse in his life, had an absolutely perfect place. Maybe Tiny should be boarding Coronado there.

Of course, where would that leave me?

Unless we could all board together, one big happy family, and she could give me lessons and I could become a great rider after years and years of klutzing around and . . .

Needless to say, in my mind's eye I was about to

ride down the center line at the Olympics when I felt something very sharp right between my shoulder blades.

A knifepoint, it had to be.

"Don't move," said a little voice. A voice I'd heard on countless tapes about dressage.

"Tiny," I said. "I—"

"And," she interrupted, poking the knife a little deeper, "don't speak."

She waited for the words to sink in.

I stood perfectly still, to indicate that they had. And I wasn't even all that worried. I mean, she was a reasonable human being and I was a reasonable human being and she obviously thought I was there to cause mayhem in some way, but hey. I'd explain and we'd even laugh about it, and we'd become good friends and . . . I was about to segue right back to my Olympic ride when she poked again.

"Turn around," she said. "And walk."

"Tiny," I began.

Poke. "No talking."

Jeez, I thought as I did her bidding. She was a heck of a lot nicer to her horse. I mean, what was this? Didn't I deserve at least the courtesy of an explanation? I mean, this was America, after all, even if it was only Bead.

"Look, I—" I tried, only to get another, wickeder poke. "Okay, I'm walking," I said, picking up the pace. "I'm walking."

I realized, as we reached the little rusted-out travel trailer, that my clothes were sopping wet.

In addition to the heat, there was my growing fear. I mean, this woman was not going to let me explain. Why was she taking me to her lair?

Suppose there really was a goddess Kehmbe. And I was to be offered up to her.

Except of course that that was stupid.

"Tiny, if you'll just—"

"Shut up," she said, raking the blade up toward my shoulder.

Ouch, I said, but in my head rather than out loud. I mean, stabbed I just didn't need.

Especially since my husband hadn't a clue about where I was.

Nobody did.

God, I thought. What if Tiny Rochambeau dropped out of sight because she'd gone stark raving mad. Like a crazed postal worker or something. What if she was out here—I don't know—lying in wait for people like me. What if, once captured, no one ever escaped from her clutches.

"Listen, you've got to let me tell you why I'm here," I blurted out.

We'd reached the door to the trailer and she reached past me and flung it open.

"Get in there," she said. "I know why you're here. And you aren't getting away with it either."

I walked into what had to be a subarctic flow of air. I mean, this air conditioner was really cranking. I even got a chill as my wet shirt all but iced over. I remembered my mother's warnings about going from one extreme of temperature to the other and thought that this time I really would get sick.

If I lived.

I was about to say something—beg and wheedle, probably—when the door to the trailer closed behind me.

I turned. And Tiny wasn't there. She'd tossed in

what I'd thought was a knife after me. It was just a broken-off whip.

Then I heard what was happening. A loud *boom boom boom*.

Tiny was nailing a board or something across the one and only door, trapping me inside.

"You can't do this," I said, hurling myself against the door, though obviously too late. "It's against the law. You can't do this to me."

There wasn't any sound from her side. Then, minutes later, I heard it: a car starting up and driving away.

I searched for a window, but there wasn't one. Just a little skylight overhead. A very little skylight. A skylight so small that even Tiny couldn't have fit through it.

Phone, I thought. Everyone has a phone. But it only took seconds to ransack the place, and guess what? Tiny wasn't everyone. Either she'd gone so off the deep end that she didn't need to communicate with anyone or she couldn't afford one.

All her money went to cool the place.

That and to buy Athlete for Coronado.

I was angry. I didn't even bother being careful as I plowed through Tiny's things. I'm not exactly sure what I was looking for—a blowtorch, maybe, to cut my way out of the joint.

Anyway, there wasn't much of anything revealing there. A television and a VCR and of course her tapes. I shuffled through the boxes and stuck one of the unlabeled ones into the machine and sat back to watch.

It was Tiny, instructing someone. I could hear her voice. I fast-forwarded a bit and here was the same someone going over some low cross-country fences.

I fast-forwarded some more. Same thing.

I ejected the tape and looked for another, stopping

when I came across one with a piece of paper rubber-banded around it.

I took it off and looked at the paper.

It bore the logo of one of the TV networks and it said: *If we'd gotten this close to the Keyes wreck, we might have used it. Too late now. Sorry.*

Following which someone's initials were scrawled.

Very chatty.

But what did it mean?

I jammed the tape in, hoping to find out, but I got so flustered thinking of what I might be about to uncover that I nearly dropped the tape while I was loading it. More than a little flustered, maybe, because I'd also started to sweat.

Oh-oh, I thought, I *am* getting sick.

But anyway, I finally got the tape in and running.

It was another lesson, this one with a rather large man.

He, too, was going over jumps, but they were all in an oval-shaped arena. There was a very posh stable in the background, too, and I recognized it as the setting for Tiny's instructional series.

Anyway, the man was going over some interesting little jumps.

I say interesting because they were made of cavalletti and arranged in a kind of zigzag pattern so that the rider would come over a zig at the trot, circle, then go over the zag, circle, etcetera, until the whole row had been traversed.

But the rider pulled up protesting, saying this was baby stuff.

I recognized him then. It was Sebastian Keyes.

Everyone knew Keyes. He was the son of a New England governor, a Yale dropout who'd moved to New York and become very flamboyant, always giving parties that were more or less bacchanals. Every-

one said his father wouldn't be reelected because of
it, but then a tragedy had occurred. Keyes had fallen
in a Long Island horse show and become paralyzed.

It was a very sad, very highly publicized thing.
Everyone but the pope had rushed to the hospital to
see Keyes. He'd been that much in the limelight, apparently.

But Tiny obviously hadn't been impressed by his
status. "Look," she was scolding him on the tape,
"I'm not going to tell you again. If you're bored, you
can take your business elsewhere."

I couldn't hear what Keyes said back, but the tone
didn't sound any less disgruntled.

"Because he *rushes*," Tiny said patiently, obviously talking about Keyes's horse. "He rushes because he's afraid. A week of this"—she gestured at
the zigzag row of jumps—"and he'll be fine."

Keyes apparently wasn't convinced. He slapped
the horse on the rump with the crop he was carrying
and took off, literally, in a cloud of dust.

Tiny turned back toward the camera, sighed re-
signedly, and said, "Good riddance, then." She
walked forward, her body filling the frame, and
then, evidently, clicked the camera off.

Phew.

I wiped the sweat off my forehead with my forearm and thought how valuable that tape probably
was; I mean, if she'd wanted to sell a video grab
from it to a tabloid or something. I mean, tabloids
were still doing features on Keyes, updates from the
rehab where he lay.

Or were they? They had been in the first month
or so after he'd crashed, but come to think of it, I
hadn't seen anything lately, so I guess it got to be
old news.

I racked my brain and couldn't even remember

what Keyes's current condition was said to be or even where he was.

And anyway, the network letter pretty much confirmed that it was too old to do stories about.

I looked around for a towel or something. I was sweating pretty heavily now. Then I noticed that the a/c had cut off.

Well, it couldn't be the electricity, I reasoned, because the VCR was still okay. But how could the a/c have conked out when, minutes before, it had been cranking like crazy?

I went over and checked the plug. Nope, it was in the socket and all. So what then?

I pulled the cover off and gasped pretty much the way the repairman who had come to Primrose Farm for the same reason—to revive an a/c that had quit—had.

I mean, don't get me wrong. I am not a super housekeeper by any means. Still, I'd never seen a wall of crud like the one inside this thing. It was worse than the wall of crud that had been on my own. I could still close my eyes and conjure up the image of that repairman wagging his finger at me and telling me that I had, through months upon months of neglect, caused my whole appliance to give up the ghost.

And Tiny evidently had done the same.

And that would explain the arctic feel of the trailer when I'd entered, too, because the repairman had told me that in its moribund state, the coils would absolutely ice over and blow colder than they'd ever blown before.

Then kaput. One dead a/c.

The diagnosis that I was able so deftly to make did not cheer me in the slightest.

But maybe there was hope.

I looked around for a sink, but there wasn't one.
Then I searched for a vacuum cleaner, again to no
avail. Finally I located a whisk broom and began
raking it along the crud-coated filter.

Nothing significant budged, but a cloud of tan
dust rose up and into my nostrils.

I sneezed about twelve times in a row, and then
had to use my arm to wipe my nose.

I was going to be a pretty sight when Tiny
Rochambeau got back. Whenever that was.

Except that without the air conditioner, the
trailer really began to heat up fast.

I mean, we're talking maybe ninety degrees.

And as hot as it was outside, very soon we'd be
talking a hundred.

Which made me beat on the unbudgeable door a
few times, just to be doing something.

Then I reassembled the air conditioner, which
still didn't work.

Great.

I began pawing through Tiny's things again, just
to be doing something, I suppose. And I came across
a manila envelope, with a message scrawled across
the outside.

Tiny, it read. *I have made copies of these.*

The message was signed by Towns.

I dumped the contents onto the floor and sat down
beside them, for a moment forgetting how sticky
and dirty and hot I was.

There was a tabloid newspaper on the top with a
picture of Sebastian Keyes. BAD COACHING RESPON-
SIBLE FOR KEYES'S PLIGHT, the headline read.

I turned to the story, which included a picture of
Tiny on the ground and Keyes, mounted, beside

her. *Coach pushed Keyes unmercifully, eyewitness says.*

The story went on about it at length, with quotes attributed to "a source close to Keyes" saying Tiny had kept urging him to jump bigger and bigger fences though Keyes himself was afraid. "His horse would rush," the source said, "but Tiny Rochambeau didn't seem to care."

I read the story in disgust—I mean, after all, I'd just seen the tape disproving the allegations. Then I flipped through the remaining stuff.

There was another article with just what I'd originally thought of—a video grab from the tape. It was the moment just before Tiny had clicked off the camera.

This huge headline said: SHARP COPY AIRS TAPE OF TINY'S RESPONSE TO KEYES TRAGEDY. Under this, in smaller, slightly different type it said: *"Good riddance," Tiny says.*

Jeez.

And there was more!

There was a letter from the company that had released Tiny's series of videotapes explaining that "under the circumstances," they were pulling them from circulation.

There were similarly phrased letters canceling clinics, too.

All the correspondence was dated about a week after the tabloid stuff—both articles and evidently the *Sharp Copy* TV show were within days of Keyes's fall.

Then I thought about Towns's message about having copies of everything.

Of course.

Towns found out that Tiny was hiding out in Bead and was about to blow her cover.

So she killed him.

CHAPTER 8

If you're trapped inside a travel trailer that is heating up rapidly, panic does not help. Panic, in fact, will probably speed your demise. This is what I told myself as I attempted to stay—metaphorically rather than literally, because literally was out of the question—cool.

Except that I'd been trapped inside by a murderess, the knowledge of which made panic a little harder to avoid.

I kept thinking about all those public-service ads about not leaving your pets inside a car because a car can heat up in minutes and cause irreversible brain damage.

And then I'd imagine God, turning the celestial oven dial to broil.

Was I hallucinating? Wasn't hallucinating a sign of impending heatstroke? Of said irreversible brain damage, in fact?

I covered my head with my hands, hoping to ward off the effects of the heat.

Then I thought, This ostrichlike behavior is getting me nowhere fast.

I scanned the room, thinking that somewhere I'd find something that would save me. And yes! There was a small brown refrigerator in the room. I staggered toward it, opened its little insulated door, and yes! A solid block of cold air hit me in the face. I started removing the contents and the single shelf. Then I stuck my head inside.

Ah!

So I wasn't going to fry after all.

In fact, the open fridge seemed to be cooling the small space—I mean the room or whatever you call the interior of a travel trailer—as a whole.

So that when Tiny came back, I'd have the energy to jump her. Jump her, and turn her over to the sheriff.

I could see Jeet's headline now:

WIFE OF EDITOR CAPTURES KILLER.

Or maybe ALLEGED KILLER. Until after the trial.

So there I was, basking in this imagined triumph when the little light in the fridge went out and the whole thing stopped making noise.

What?

Had I blown a fuse?

I looked around, but didn't see anything resembling a fuse box.

I tried the VCR, and it, too, was dead. So there wasn't any electricity, for sure.

Except that there had to be a way of turning the power back on. Because without it, I was going to fry.

I searched all available wall surfaces and all along the floor, too.

Nada.

Then I saw it, sort of smirking up at me from the kitchen counter: an overdue notice from the electric company. I read the disconnect date.

Today.

So even if the a/c hadn't crapped out, I'd have been out of luck. The question was, though, did Tiny know? Was she deliberately trying to kill me, too?

Because the trailer was heating up again, and faster than I'd have believed. But of course, at this time of day, it had to be nearly a hundred degrees outside.

This time of day! I looked at my watch. Although the recent cold air had fogged the lens, I could still read the time: 3:15.

Oh, no.

That meant I'd missed the time I was supposed to feed.

Which also meant that if I survived Tiny, Booger would kill me.

But this was no joking matter. I mean, I knew that eventually someone would come along and discover I wasn't there and feed Plum and Spier, surely. But how would anyone, save Tiny, discover me?

I had to live. I had to get out of this place. I had to . . .

Liquids, I thought, examining the rapidly warming contents of the little fridge.

Six bottles of Gatorade. No wonder Tiny was so tiny. And she probably didn't have an electrolyte problem either.

They were small bottles, though. Sports bottles, the label said.

I took one, and pulled and tugged and yanked and twisted. Still, no matter what I did, I couldn't get the blankety-blank thing to open. What was this? A childproof bottle or something? God forbid some ten-year-old should overdose.

But by this time I'd managed to wrench off the cellophane and had reached the cuplike plastic thing that went over the mouth of the bottle. I could see the squisher thing inside.

Relax, I told myself.

Then the cup was off.

Phew.

I held the bottle up to my mouth and sucked.

Nothing.

"It's broken or something," I said out loud, shaking it. Then I banged it, squisher down, against the floor.

Not a drop of the amber-colored fluid escaped.

What was this? I was going to die of thirst with a bottle that could save me in my very hand?

I turned it upside down and sucked harder, louder, but no.

Finally I thought to unscrew the entire squisher mechanism. And there I was, staring at a foil seal that kept the liquid inside.

Damn! What were these packaging people down at Gatorade worried about? I mean, do you have to have an engineering degree to enjoy a simple drink? I mean, especially when your life is depending on it, which mine did appear to be.

I drank the Gatorade and felt a little less furious, but not much.

The second bottle, which I managed to open right out of the chute, made me feel a wee bit better. Physically and in terms of my spirits, too.

Still, what is the reason for that? I mean, I can see some really stupid jogger actually perishing while clutching a plastic bottle whose mysteries he wasn't able to plumb.

We're talking major lawsuit here. Or at the very least News of the Weird.

I stood up and looked in a mirror that was hanging over a cutting board, stunned by how red my face was. I shouldn't have been surprised, though. I mean, I was maybe fifteen minutes away from a roaring headache. The kind I get when I've been out in the sun too long. And I know, you're thinking

that I wasn't out in the sun now, but I might as well
have been, what with the way it was bearing down
on the flat trailer roof. In fact, it was probably worse
in here than it was out there.

I tried to talk myself into attempting a siesta, if
only to shut down the systems of my body. But
right. Like I was going to be able to sleep while
steaming like a broccoli floret inside some mad-
woman's trailer. In the middle of nowhere. Without
anyone in the world having a clue as to where to
find me.

All of a sudden I thought of Della and Jeet and
how worried they would be. They'd have come out of
Della's office by now, of course, and they would have
looked around for me. And then what? Where would
Jeet think I'd gone?

What would he do? Call the incompetent sheriff?

I looked around for something to fan myself with.
Wasn't there a bathtub I could sit in? A toilet I could
use as a sink?

Sink!

I hadn't found one earlier, but I'd dismissed the
cutting board. But what do you usually put your cutting board over? What did Jeet put his over?

The sink!

I staggered over to it and hurled the cutting board
aside. And there it was, one of those squirter things
that apparently subbed for a faucet. I was saved. I
pressed. Yes! Tepid water spewed from it. I put my
head underneath it until the flow had stopped.

I kept pressing.

Nothing.

Then I looked below.

It was a tank rather than an actual plumbing
hookup as we know it.

An empty tank now.

I sank to the floor and started crying. Then I wondered if the loss of tears would dehydrate me even further.

My God, I thought. Tiny was living in primitive conditions, not being able to pay her bills in order to hang on to that dressage horse of hers. What did she do when she had to go to the bathroom? Make like a bear? Except that I don't know what I'd have done to hang on to Plum and Spier. Plenty, probably. And so, even though she was a murderer, I felt a kind of kinship with her. I mean, she couldn't be all bad, right?

Except that I could picture the street corner where she'd nailed Towns. He'd have been jogging in place, probably, waiting for her to drive past. Maybe he couldn't even see her behind the wheel in the predawn light.

She'd wave him on.

He'd wave back, grateful, and start diagonally across the street.

And then she'd gun her Lamborghini and slam into him.

There'd be the small, crumpling sound. Towns's body would go up, up, into the air as if he were springing off a trampoline. Then it would slam to the pavement.

And Tiny would go blithely on her way, maybe not even looking in the rearview mirror.

What had DeWitt told me? Something about how Towns had one enemy for sure. And that was Tiny. It had to be.

Except that I'd have to forget the Lamborghini. Towns had probably died with—what color was that Toyota, anyway?—a mixture of primer and Bondo all over his jogging shorts.

What had it been like for Towns, in those last

seconds, when he realized she was gunning the engine and coming for him? And had he died all at once, or had he lain there, eyes on the sky, dying as the light came brighter and brighter.

I lay back, staring at the skylight, my spirit merging with the departed Towns's. I wished I hadn't eaten all that I'd eaten in my lifetime so that I could fit through the little skylight in the trailer's rooftop.

Well.

I think you know the state I was in, the slide I was making toward unconsciousness and maybe even death. Even I knew it.

I had stopped sweating, for instance. My skin was hot and dry. And my mind kept drifting. . . .

I tried to remember anything I'd read about heat prostration, but I couldn't. All I could remember was stuff I'd learned about riding.

I don't mean heavy-duty stuff. I mean beginner stuff. Like how to post on the correct diagonal. I was remembering not being able to get that, when to bob up and when to sit down, and thinking, This is it. As much as I want to ride, I will never be able to master this, and then, voilà! I got it. I got it and to this day I don't even have to think about it. I just do it naturally. I start on the correct diagonal, and I change diagonals when I change direction, and I can tell what diagonal I'm on without looking down at the horse's shoulder.

And so there I was, on the floor of Tiny Rochambeau's travel trailer, smiling. Congratulating myself for all this. And in my fevered mind posting.

Watching myself post, watching how low and how efficiently I could do it, when I heard a kind of tearing, wrenching sound, and the trailer shook a little, and I thought I could hear Spier beating his shod hooves against the side of it the way he would the trough.

I was pretty far gone.

Then the door groaned open and a shaft of sunlight fell across my body and I was dragged into the midafternoon Texas heat, which, in comparison with the inside of that little trailer, felt positively subzero.

A big fat finger wagged in my face, so close that I couldn't bring it into focus, but I didn't care. I was trotting Plum across a huge floe of white ice, posting to beat the band. Plum's mane was flying and crystals of ice were flaking off it and hitting me in the face. I could hear whinnying in the distance and, right in front of me, a human voice berating me, saying that I couldn't be trusted worth a damn.

I tried to protest, but my lips seemed sealed shut. I wasn't posting anymore. I wasn't even on Plum—I was on the ground.

Had I fallen off?

I started to whimper when someone slapped me across the face. "Oh, no you don't," a voice said. "You ain't dying just yet."

CHAPTER 9

And then I was lying out on the grass and I was slapping at the fire ants who had discovered me and my sodden clothing and I was staring up at two pretty hideous faces:

One was the feed-store clerk's.

The other was Booger's.

I think that's when I wished I'd pass out or at least reenter the delirium from which I'd just emerged.

Booger was back to finger wagging and he was reiterating what he'd said about me not being trustworthy. "You said you'd feed at three," he kept saying. "You held your hand up like it was a pledge. And it turned out your word wasn't worth a damn."

I batted at my right arm, which was being stung by ants.

"See there?" the clerk said. "She's okay. She's aware of them ants."

"She pretty well damn better be aware," Booger said. He was glaring down at me, still with less-than-friendly intent. "You better be glad you asked me about this lady with the coal-black hair, else I wouldn't have found you."

"I seen her drive this way, though," the clerk, eager to claim his share in my rescue, added.

"But you ain't gonna get away with them horses

of yours waking me up the way they did," Booger insisted.

Mercifully, however, there was a big paper cup that said DAIRY QUEEN on it beside him, and he dipped down into it and tossed some bits of rapidly dissolving ice in my face. It felt just the way the flecks of ice breaking off from Plum's mane had, only wetter.

"Aw, take it easy on her," the clerk urged.

Yeah, I said inside. But I still couldn't make the word surface. My throat felt frozen, paralyzed. Like Sebastian Keyes's throat, I thought. Or Towns's.

And then, although I'd have sworn there wasn't any liquid left inside my body, I started to cry again, more uncontrollably than I had when I was trapped inside alone.

"Oh, no you don't," Booger shouted. "You ain't pullin' that girlie stuff on me."

"Let her be," the clerk said, "for now."

"That's easy for you to say," Booger complained. "You don't need your daytime sleep."

"Oh, come on, Boog," the clerk said. "Seems like you was mighty glad to have an excuse to come on out here."

I was looking up at Booger's face, which of course was looming just inches above my own. So I saw his reaction, which was to go from a sort of general apoplectic pink to a bright, hard lobster red.

"You shut your mouth," Booger said. "Else I'll shut it for you."

I would have found the experience unpleasant beyond words except for one thing: Booger was now holding the cup, which was ice-cold from the melting ice inside it—against my forehead.

The water that was dripping from it—condensation, I suppose—was luscious and cool. I gratefully lifted my head as much as I could toward the cup and ceased

to care about why they were there or what Booger was
so angry about.

I'd be able to talk soon, I realized, as my throat
and probably my body temperature began to return
to normal. I'd be able to tell them about Tiny. About
her killing Towns and closing me inside the Trailer
from Hell.

And forget that disconnect notice from the electric
company. I wouldn't mention anything that would
make her argue that the whole thing had been acci-
dental. I had come around to believing—about the
time the temperature inside her place went over a
hundred degrees—that she'd zapped the electricity
on purpose. And anyway, she'd nailed me inside. Unless she got Johnny Cochran and Alan Dershowitz to
defend her, I felt I could make a pretty strong case.

Then the clerk nudged Booger in the ribs and Booger
reddened—if you can imagine this—even more. "Here
she comes," the clerk said. "Here comes Miss Tiny."

Booger looked around, presumably for her, and
then back at me.

"Fooled you," the clerk said, smiling and showing
all his wacky teeth.

I thought, My God, Booger is sweet on the woman.

And then I thought, But she's lethal.

And then, A match made in heaven.

Depleted as I was, I heard myself chuckling
softly. "You're sweet on Tiny," I croaked, clutching Booger's blue-chambrayed sleeve.

Booger yanked his arm away so suddenly that
I wouldn't have been surprised to see my fin-
gernails still embedded in the fabric of his shirt. Instead, they stayed where they belonged, and ached.

I discovered I was able to say, "Hey!" in a fairly
loud tone and pull myself up to one elbow.

Booger moved in front of me, blocking practically

all else from view. "You said you would feed at three o'clock on the nose," he kept harping. "Here it is, the first day out of the chute, and you didn't do it. First day!"

"I was . . ." I began, but my voice gave way. But anyway, didn't the man know I had been trapped inside an overheated trailer? Hadn't he rescued me himself? I mean, surely there are some acceptable reasons for not showing up.

"Aw, tell her what you done to them horses," the feed clerk said.

"What?" I sat bolt upright, which made the world spin. But what did the feed clerk mean? Had Booger shot them, or what? I battled the dizziness and rose to my knees.

"Tell her, Boog," the clerk urged.

Booger mumbled, but I heard what he said. "I fed 'em both," he said, embarrassed to have done something nice. "Grained 'em and gave them hay and cold water both."

I found my voice again. It still scratched against my throat, but I managed to say, "Thanks."

"But that don't mean I want to hear excuses," Booger screamed anew. "Damned horses woke me up. I told you, I work nights and I need my sleep."

He turned to the clerk and bellowed an explanation. "Damned horses, both of 'em, banging on that trough to beat the band. I tell you, they liked to raise the dead, those two. It was like . . . it was like . . ." He paused to catch his breath and think of a likely comparison.

Then he had it. "It was like one of them headache commercials on TV," he said. "It was like a riot in Cell Block B. It was like . . ."

But I didn't have to hear another analogy. No. Because we were interrupted by the squeal of brakes.

It was Tiny, skidding to a stop in the trashed-out, gunshot Toyota coupe that I'd seen on the way in. It looked as if it had been rolled, and more than once, too. I couldn't believe it was roadworthy.

The change in Booger was instantaneous. He stopped shouting. He gulped. He began slicking his hair back, first with one hand, then the other. His voice dropped into a deeper, I suppose he thought seductive, register. "Of course I probably underfed. Gave them half a coffee can apiece." He smiled, the soul of neighborliness and generosity.

Then he stood up and moved off way to the side, assuming an aw-shucks pose.

Tiny, meanwhile, strode over to where we had clustered. "What happened?" she asked.

Oh, right. Like she didn't know.

"The electricity went out and I all but fricasseed," I said, standing for the first time. The world wobbled and threatened to whirl, but then stood still. "I could have died," I told her. I don't think I sounded as if I'd been amused by the experience.

"Oh, God," she said, pretending to be horrified.

Right. Like she nails me in and then expresses surprise.

And fortunately she wasn't going to get away with it. No sir. Driving in, lickety-split, was the sheriff's bubble top. The sheriff himself arrived in a cloud of dust, though without the hearty hi-oh-Silver.

"Sheriff," I said, moving toward him, but he pretty much ignored me, speaking instead to Tiny. He did take out his handcuffs, though.

"Think I need to cuff her?" he asked.

I was about to say, *Well, of course you do, you nincompoop. She's a murderer, isn't she?* when I realized he was talking about cuffing me.

Me!

"I don't know," Tiny said. "She's been in the heat and she's probably . . ."

Me!

"Well, it's your horse she was trying to steal," the sheriff said.

My mouth fell open.

"I know," Tiny said, "but she's been in that heat."

"But sheriff, she—" I began.

"Excuse me," he said pointedly, indicating the cuffs. It was a threat if I ever saw one.

I got the picture. I stepped out of the way. I mean, this could turn ugly. And there were enough people here, probably, to hold me down.

Except that I was starting to formulate a plan. Because indeed, all I could think of to do to save my neck in a situation as upsetting as this one was get to my husband, Jeet.

He wouldn't let them railroad me like this. Get to my husband, and if I needed to, get him to break the news in the paper. The truth. That Tiny had murdered Towns and that she'd tried, also, to kill me.

"Nobody would ever believe I'm a horse thief," I said belligerently.

"I suppose that's why you brought your horse trailer with you when you come," the sheriff said.

"Look." I tried to sound reasonable. "Tiny is a murderer. She killed Towns."

"Sheriff," Booger broke in, and pointed at me. "I know this woman here and you just plumb can't believe a word she says. Plus everybody who knows Tiny here . . ." He ducked his head and blushed furiously before glancing at Tiny and resuming. "Well, everybody who knows Tiny knows how sweet she is and all."

"Well, thank you," Tiny simpered.

And the next thing you know, here they were, this farmer from Nowhere, Texas, and this international dressage figure, smiling at each other like high-school sophomores at the hop.

Go figure.

Except that I wasn't about to take the fall for attempting to steal Coronado. I didn't even know where Coronado was! Last time I'd seen him, he had just about dumped Tiny and run off, and then, after she'd regained herself, she'd ridden him into the woods.

I said as much.

"Oh," Tiny said, with an air of just having put two and two together, "*you're* the reason he freaked."

"What do you mean?" the sheriff asked her.

"She frightened my horse and I almost fell off."

"Hmmm." The sheriff scratched his chin. "Seems like it might be a form of assault."

It sounded more like Bead justice to me. And it was something I couldn't afford.

I looked at Tiny. She was wearing a one-piece riding thing. I mean, one of those Lycra jobs that molds to your body.

She had no pockets, no lumps anywhere to be seen.

She wasn't carrying a purse.

That meant just one thing: the keys to the Toyota were probably still in the car. I could just about visualize them dangling from the ignition. So if I could sprint to the car and take off before the sheriff could unholster his big silver pistol . . .

But sprinting would require a thrust of energy I wasn't sure I had. I visualized my old gym teacher, Miss Barr, spurring me on on the lacrosse field. "Are you committed?" she would yell, and suddenly we were.

And then I could hear them all yelling behind me—Tiny and the sheriff and Booger and the feed-store clerk. Yelling things like "Hey!" and "Stop her!" and "You won't get away with this."

My life as a fugitive Toyota thief had begun.

CHAPTER 10

I bounced up the driveway like a Ping-Pong ball, and was tooling down the highway now, making better time than I'd have thought possible in a car like the one I was driving.

All those years in Mother had apparently stood me in good stead. I even managed to shift, although the gearshift stick in the Toyota was broken off, maybe only half a stick, and with no handle or knob to hang on to.

But compared with driving an old monster truck and a great big long trailer, cornering in the little car, even one pitted out the way this one was, was a snap.

I was actually enjoying it—the thrill of having made a daring escape and all. Of course, I was pretty much able to enjoy it because I knew that once I got to Jeet, island of sanity that he was, everything would be all right. And he'd be able to get the truth out. I had the power of the press behind me. I was a lucky woman indeed.

Then my luck ran out.

The sheriff had obviously radioed ahead and a roadblock had been erected.

Two police cars with bubble tops sat on the road-

side, and a guy in a fluorescent vest was waving his
arms for me to stop.

I stopped.

He came up to the car. He was wearing civvies
underneath the vest, I noticed.

I held my hands over my head. "Okay, okay," I
said. "But I need to explain." I was about to tell him
that while, yes, I *did* steal the car, it was under
duress. Because I'd been falsely accused of having
tried to steal a horse. When meanwhile, what had
really happened was that a murderess had tried to
add me to her list. And anyway, if I really were a car
thief, would I steal a car like *this*?

Before I could utter a word, the man pushed a
clipboard through the window of the car.

Ha!

He hadn't read me my rights. I'd watched enough
television to know what that meant. It meant they
wouldn't be able to make any charges—which I as-
sume now meant grand theft auto in addition to
grand theft horse—against me stick.

And handing me a printed copy of said rights
wouldn't count for anything either, because for all
this man knew, I could be illiterate. I wouldn't need
O.J.'s defense team for this one.

"Ha-ha," I said. "You didn't read me my rights."

The guy looked puzzled. "No," he said, "you're the
one who's supposed to read. This is a petition." He
gestured at the clipboard that was now balanced on
the steering wheel.

"Petition? What about the police cars?"

"Oh," he said. "They're so things stay peaceable."

"You mean I'm not under arrest?" I asked.

"Why would you be?" he asked.

I looked in my rearview mirror. I didn't see the
sheriff's car yet, but it was bound to appear any sec-

ond now. I peeled out, leaving big thick smears of rubber on the pavement, I'm sure.

"Hey!" the guy yelled. "You can't take that!"

Was this grand theft clipboard?

I thought about throwing the clipboard out the window, but I wasn't sure it wouldn't be ruined if I did that. I would just have to return it later. Meanwhile I had bigger fish to fry, in that I had to get to Jeet and the newspaper office and relative safety.

Whew! Thank God that Booger had fed Plum and Spier for me, or in the middle of all of this I'd have had to go over there and do that as well. Booger was all right after all. Pity he'd fallen for Tiny Hit-and-Run Rochambeau.

I spied the turnoff that I wanted and squealed onto it.

I was minutes from my goal.

Still, I couldn't relax, because for all I knew, the sheriff was entitled to shoot me on sight for having fled the scene of my own arrest.

Oy.

I hid the Toyota behind the newspaper's Dumpster, then snatched up the clipboard and hurled myself into the offices of *The Bead Weekly*.

A deathly quiet prevailed.

"Jeet?" I called.

Nothing.

I glanced at the clock. It was after five. Perhaps he'd gone out for a bite.

And without me. Phooey.

I read the petition while I waited hopefully.

It was about the graveyard, Bucking Hill, which allegedly was one of the last remaining burial sites kept in the traditional way.

Hmmm.

I read on to discover that the traditional way was what I'd first found so startling about the place: it was kept free of grass, raked, in fact, with mounds indicating grave sites.

And somebody wanted to tear the place up because there was a hot spring bubbling practically beneath it.

The petition concluded by saying that if Towns Loving were alive, there'd be no such movement, because he would have crusaded against it. *Sign it for Towns,* the document urged.

And there was something there, too, about that house beyond the graveyard—the house where I'd first seen the Tony Perkins look-alike. It apparently was, if the graveyard were successfully moved, slated to become a resort hotel.

WE DON'T NEED THIS IN BEAD!!! the petitioner had written.

Well, here was yet another story for Jeet.

He could write it right after the one about me being falsely accused of trying to steal Tiny Rochambeau's horse.

And he could write that one on the heels of the lead story, which of course would be about Tiny Rochambeau confessing to murder.

Which, for all I knew, she had. I mean, where was she if the sheriff wasn't booking her? Because surely Booger and the clerk were telling him about the way I'd been found. I couldn't have nailed myself inside that trailer of hers.

Except that Booger was so gaga in her presence, he probably didn't even remember having to unhammer several nails in order to get to me.

And if Tiny had local roots—because why else would she be here, for God's sake?—and was going to press this idiotic thing about me being after Coronado, she just might get pretty far with it.

Except that if she were planning to do that, why hadn't she and the sheriff shown up?

Because you'd have to be pretty dumb not to be able to find me, a total stranger, in Bead. I mean, I *still* didn't know where Jeet and I were living. So where else could I be but here, at the offices of *The Bead Weekly*?

Come *on*, Jeet, I mentally urged his return. It did seem as though he was taking a pretty long coffee break. Unless, of course, he was out trolling the streets for me.

But no, he'd have left a note on the door in case I showed up here. Jeet was like that, cautious and clever. He wouldn't just go off the way I would.

I had to keep myself busy and wait, that was all. Because even if the sheriff came to arrest me, once Jeet turned up, everything would be okay.

But actually, if the sheriff had even half a brain, he'd have Tiny in custody and would be coming to me to get a statement.

Ha! Take that, bitch, I thought, squirreling up my face at an imaginary Tiny.

I found myself thinking back to the events of the afternoon, Booger's rescue in particular. It was the horses who had actually saved me. The horses, Plum and Spier, who, by alerting Booger to my absence, had sent him to Tiny's in search of me. And whew! Thank goodness I'd asked him about her.

I was already composing a headline:

HORSES SAVE LIFE OF EDITOR'S WIFE.

Or HORSES SAVE LIFE OF TEMPORARY EDITOR'S WIFE.

Hmmm. I'd have to check with Jeet about the finer stylistic points of headline composition. It could be that, if the sentence were parsed by a strict sort of person, I'd be calling myself Jeet's temporary wife.

Sentences are like that.

But anyway, however the story read, it would be sure to make the residents of Bead sleep a little easier. Because a murderer would very soon no longer be roaming their streets. A murderer—in the small and elegant form of Tiny Rochambeau—was about to find herself where she belonged: behind bars.

Jeet would see to that.

I saw a flash of white outside in the parking lot. The trousers of Boone DeWitt. He was arguing with his wife, and even though I couldn't hear a word, I could tell from their gestures what the argument was about. He wanted to come inside the building, and she didn't think he should.

My first instinct was to think, Poor Boone, but then I thought, Hey. People almost always marry the kind of people they want to marry. I don't know how many times I've felt sorry for someone for being tangled up with some really horrible person only to discover, guess what? That they *love* that person. That they *chose* that person and that it wasn't as though the person had pretended to be somebody else. No. They *liked* something about the very person that I didn't.

I don't claim to be the greatest judge of character, okay?

I watched, though, as June DeWitt won out and began leading her husband away.

I realized then, too, how much I would have liked company right then. Yes, even theirs.

Where was everyone, anyway? I wondered, standing at the long slanted table where they apparently pasted the newspaper together. I say apparently, because there were things like scissors and glue sticks and rulers and X-Acto knives—those wicked little penlike jobs with the razors in the head for blades.

I picked up one of the long, slender reporter notepads I'd seen Jeet use. The kind I'd used when I'd gone along with Boone DeWitt—gosh, not so many hours ago.

So much had gone on!

I wrote: HORSES ALERT MAN TO . . . and then crossed it out.

I tried: HORSES UNEARTH . . . and scrapped it, too.

Then: HORSES SOLVE MURDER . . . and stood back to look at it. It was a promising start.

. . . OF TOWNS LOVING, I added. And there it was, the perfect head: HORSES SOLVE MURDER OF TOWNS LOVING. I wrote it on a fresh page, in letters as big as the notepad would allow, and held it at arm's length to admire it.

I got so absorbed in this that I didn't hear her come up behind me. When she spoke, I jumped.

"So," she said, "the murder has been solved."

I caught my breath and then laughed. "God, Della. You scared me half to death," I said. Then I recovered, and grew somber. I mean, after all, she'd been married to Towns, so this had to be a major moment for her. "It's true, though. All I have to do is tell Jeet so that the sheriff can arrest—"

I stopped because she'd reached up, clutched her heart, and sort of swayed. The only thing I could think of was that she was having a heart attack. I held my arms out, hoping to grab her before she fell, and she pulled back and away, as if I'd been trying to harm her.

I guess when someone in your family has been murdered, you might react that way. But what about closure? Aren't family members supposed to be glad in some deep, primal way when the person who has bumped off their loved one is brought to justice? Or about to be?

"Della . . ." I began, walking toward her.

She kept shaking her head, no, no, no, and backing away.

But I had more immediate problems, cruel as it sounds to say. I had to save my own skin, and that meant finding Jeet. And Della didn't seem to want to hear about the murder being solved anyway, so I changed the subject.

"Della," I asked, "where in the blazes is Jeet?"

Before she could answer, there was a squeal of brakes outside. We both looked up to see the sheriff.

He was with Tiny Rochambeau. And she obviously hadn't confessed, because she wasn't handcuffed.

The two of them burst through the door, side by side.

Della's lower lip quivered, and she said, "This is an outrage." It was almost as if she knew they'd come to arrest me and knew, too, how really stupid that was.

And that could be. The sheriff could have called the paper while I was on the road and alerted Della to all that had gone on. I stepped in front of Della, eager to argue my case now that I was certain she was on my side.

"I did not try to steal your horse," I said to Tiny. Then, to the sheriff, I added, "And I had no choice but to take the car. And anyway"—I looked toward Tiny again—"she's a murderer. She killed Towns and even tried—"

A sort of strangled sob from Della stopped me from going on.

I saw the sheriff's eyes, and Tiny's, too, go wide. They apparently felt I'd spoken too callously or something.

I turned.

Della's eyes were—I don't know—evil. And they were trained full bore on Tiny, too.

"It's all right, Del," I said, catching hold of her arm. "I can handle this myself."

Della turned her gaze on me. I withered beneath it. Had she gone bonkers? Did she think I was the one who had mowed her husband down in the street? I mean, she was looking at me as though she was about to tear my heart out with her bare hands.

I was wedged up against one of the old wooden desks, so there wasn't anything for me to do but stand there until—whew!—she stopped looking at me like that and turned back toward Tiny.

Do you know what a tableau is, where everyone is kind of frozen in place? I guess a freeze-frame in a movie would be the contemporary equivalent.

Well, there we all were, in freeze-frame.

And I hadn't even had a chance to tell the sheriff what Tiny had done to me, barricading me inside that trailer of hers either. That woman was dangerous, and something had to be done about it, I decided, even if it did mean bruising poor Della's feelings by being blunt.

"Sheriff," I said, pointing past Del at Tiny. "I demand that you arrest her for Towns Loving's murder right this minute."

CHAPTER 11

I told you we had all been frozen there. Which is probably why none of us had time to react.

When Della started toward Tiny, I mean.

I know the sheriff was totally taken off guard, because although he'd reached down toward his gun, he didn't unholster it. He just kept his hand there by it as Della jerked Tiny toward herself.

She spun Tiny around as though the two of them had rehearsed the move. Then she pulled Tiny's arm back the way wrestlers do, in a hammerlock, I think it's called.

Kids do it to each other all the time and it hurts fiercely.

You'd never know it hurt, though, to look at Tiny's face. It betrayed nothing beyond interest.

And why should it? She was a cold-blooded killer, after all.

"Della," I said softly. Maybe too softly, because no one acted as though I'd said a word. "Della, of course you're mad. And we understand. Really. We do."

I looked to the sheriff for confirmation, but he didn't say a thing. He was watching hungrily. The way you'd expect a man to watch bearbaiting or some other equally savage pursuit. No kidding, he was even licking his lips.

I wanted to sock him. I mean, this was all his fault. If he'd gone and arrested Tiny, then she'd be safely behind bars and Della wouldn't be putting herself in maybe legal jeopardy by trying to beat up the woman who'd killed her husband.

God, that sheriff ought to be impeached! Had Bead elected him? I mean, were people, even here in Bead, that dumb?

I pointed. "Sheriff, you know damn well that she killed Towns. Now, why haven't you arrested her?" I sounded like a little kid who was squealing on a chum, but at this point I didn't care.

And then I got the shock of my life.

Because Della, still holding Tiny's arm back in the one-move-and-I'll-snap-it-off pose with her left hand, groped around on the layout table with her right and picked up one of the X-Acto knives I told you about. The ones with the little razor at the tip?

They're scalpels, really.

The blade flashed silver. And guess where. At Tiny's throat.

"Great," I muttered. I sighed in deep disgust. Because now Della could be charged with assault, I'll bet.

And who could blame her? She was in the same room with Tiny, the woman who had wrenched her husband away from her, and the sheriff, apparently, was going to let this Tiny person go free. Well, jeez.

I stepped toward Della and her victim. "Del," I said, trying to inject some sense into the situation. I did, however, try to speak euphemistically so as not to upset poor Del even more. "Del. We know that Tiny took Towns away from you, but—"

Della's voice turned deep, the way Linda Blair's had in *The Exorcist*. "She did," Della intoned. "She took him away."

The sheriff had a hand in his pocket now. Right. Time to chill out and relax.

But Tiny, I've got to hand it to her, stayed really cool.

And why wouldn't she? She was, after all, in addition to the cold-blooded-killer thing, a very tough rider. A very tough trainer. A very tough coach. Not foolhardy and irresponsible, the way that newspaper article that had been done on her said, but tough the way you have to be with horses.

In fact, I remember her saying on a video I'd rented that tough is what it took. Lola and I sat laughing about the way she'd expressed it. "When a horse pulls his .357 Magnum out," she'd said, "and when you're asking him to do really athletic stuff that he doesn't want to do, he *will* pull it out, you have to take out your Uzi. Because if you don't take out your Uzi, then next thing you know, you'll be cringing whenever he reaches for his pocket."

So Tiny didn't bat an eye at Della and the blade. But she didn't take her Uzi out, either. Instead, she stood stock-still, following the movements of Della's scalpel-waving hand the way a charmer follows the movements of a snake.

Or is it the other way around?

Della, meanwhile, wanted to rile Tiny. You could tell. "You bitch," Della said, her voice as deep as a man's.

Tiny was silent.

"You thought I didn't know," Della said.

Well, my interest was certainly piqued. What did this mean? That Della knew all along that Tiny was the killer?

I looked from Del to the sheriff, and though he

didn't look puzzled, he wasn't about to come forward with a satisfying explanation, either.

"Admit it," Della said, referring to God knows what.

Tiny didn't.

The blade came very close to the corner of Tiny's eye.

And Tiny didn't even blink.

"How often did you see each other?" Della asked. "Once, twice a week? How often?"

I thought, Oh.

Tiny frowned. I saw her swallow. I wasn't sure that Della did, though. To Della, she may have seemed totally cool.

Della let go of Tiny's arm and walked around Tiny, assessing her little boy's figure. The flat breasts, the almost nonexistent hips. "I wouldn't have thought he'd like your type," Della said, gesturing with her free hand, though still menacing Tiny with the X-Acto knife with the other.

The sheriff was now giving Della, a former Miss Macon, remember, an appreciative once-over.

It was pretty disgusting.

But *were* Towns and Tiny having an affair? Then why would he be out to expose Tiny? Did they have a lovers' tiff, maybe?

"You thought you'd get away with it, didn't you?" Della said.

Tiny let out an exasperated—and under the circumstances, ballsy—sigh.

And that's when Della, at least momentarily, lost it.

She grabbed Tiny's arm again, stepping back and hammerlocking it once more. This time she was pulling really hard, making Tiny wince.

Tiny shut her eyes. Tears seeped out from under her eyelids.

With her free hand, Della held the tiny blade against Tiny's small, white throat. "I told you, bitch," she said. "I want you to admit it. I want to know."

A thin red line appeared on Tiny's neck.

Blood.

I figured that if Tiny didn't say something soon, she'd end up getting seriously hurt. I mean, an X-Acto knife is a tiny thing, but so is the carotid artery, if you think about it. So that even though Tiny was guilty, she should live for either the confession or the trial, don't you think?

Tiny evidently knew that, too. She swallowed once, and then began to speak. Her voice, unlike my own in dire circumstances, betrayed nothing in the way of fear. It was clipped and businesslike, exactly the voice on her instructional videos.

"My reputation had been ruined," Tiny said evenly. "I came here, to the newspaper, for help. Your husband was intrigued by my story—by the way my seemingly solid business had been ruined by the Sebastian Keyes accident. By the distortions in the press and with the very videotape I'd hoped would salvage things. Towns was planning to write a rebuttal. He was a wonderful man, Towns. He was going to help me."

"I don't believe you," Della responded, jerking upward on Tiny's arm.

Tiny gasped with the sudden pain. "It's true," she said. "A tabloid had done a story about me. A story that was quite unfair. Unfair and untrue. Towns said he could set things right."

Della eased up just a bit. You could see that she recognized her husband's character in what Tiny Rochambeau was saying.

But Del didn't give up that easily. She yanked on

Tiny some more. "You didn't sleep together?" she demanded, her eyes hardening. She aimed the very tip of the X-Acto blade at the throbbing vein on the side of Tiny's neck as she spoke.

"No," Tiny said.

"Never?"

"No," Tiny said again.

"Then why was he going to leave me?" Della shrieked. "Why?"

The sheriff and I looked at each other in an unexpected moment of understanding. Because you're a bitch, Della, we were both thinking. Because he'd had you up to here.

Della pulled the blade back, not as if she were planning to stop, but as if she were going to plunge it into Tiny all the way.

I know my heart stopped beating. I think the same was true for even the sheriff.

Except at that precise moment, the air conditioner, the throbbing heart of the universe, kicked itself on with a sound so deafening that Della, who apparently had never stood directly below the ventilation shaft, jerked violently.

In the process, she dropped the weapon.

The sheriff had it before it could bounce.

Out of nowhere, June DeWitt came hurtling into the room and landed on top of Della, pinning her facedown on the layout table in what can only be described as a full-body slam.

"Get off of me," Della was squealing, except that her voice was muffled by virtue of having to be heard through the whole of June's Valkyrie frame.

Boone DeWitt came rushing into the room behind her, a camera up to his face. The flash went off three times in a row, like a strobe. "I've got it," he kept yelling. "I've got it."

"And I've got her," the sheriff said, tapping June on the shoulder. When June DeWitt finally stood aside, he clamped a pair of handcuffs on Della.

Tiny leaned against the slanted table, rubbing her throat.

I was confused.

Until Della looked me straight in the eye and said, "I killed him for nothing. Can you believe that? I killed poor Towns for absolutely nothing."

The sheriff pulled one of those palm-sized tape recorders out of his pocket. He spooled it backward a hair, then forward again. We all listened as Della, on tape, said she'd killed poor Towns.

Then the sheriff, tape still rolling, read Della her rights.

"Don't you people be going anywhere, hear?" he said. "I'll need statements from you all. But first let me take care of Miss Della here."

He led her, gallantly, I thought, out toward the bubble top in the parking lot.

It was a lot to assimilate, but Tiny helped me by explaining. She and Towns had been meeting, sometimes several nights a week. "He really was a good man," she said.

She'd come to Bead because it was a refuge. "I remembered it from the time I was a little girl," she said. Her grandparents had lived on the land she was now inhabiting with Coronado.

"I wasn't trying to steal your horse," I said, when she mentioned him.

Before Tiny could say she was sorry for even accusing me, Booger came stumbling into the room. He had a rifle cradled at his side. "I watched it all," he told Tiny. "Another second and I'd have blown her away."

Tiny smiled and looked oddly embarrassed.

"I know I'm not much," Booger said, standing in front of her, "but I'll treat you good. I fixed a place up for your horse and all. All I ask is that you give me a chance. I've been watching you, over at the feed store and all. I've been watching you and thinking how I'd like to make a home for you and your horse."

So that explained his place.

Tiny tilted her head shyly. She seemed to be considering it.

But then Tiny was apologizing to me, and about more than the horse. She was saying that she'd had no idea that the electric company was going to cut her off and Booger was saying that if she accepted his hand in marriage, she'd never have to worry about another bill for as long as she lived.

In the background, Boone DeWitt was on the phone asking for the area code for Lantana, Florida, and then he was yelling about the pictures he had of a murderer being captured.

June, the Valkyrie, listening to Boone on the horn, seemed, well, adoring. As adoring as a Valkyrie can be. She said, "I didn't think journalism would be this exciting." And then she flexed a biceps and said something about studying martial arts.

And all of a sudden I thought again of Jeet.

Where *was* he?

Then I had a little clutch of fear. Because I'd last seen him alone with Della.

Della, whom I now knew was a crazed killer.

CHAPTER 12

"Has anyone seen Jeet?" I asked. I wasn't really panicked. I mean, the chances of Della having done him in seemed, even in the light of what I'd learned about her, unlikely.

And every other time I'd thought the worst regarding Jeet, I'd been wrong.

I mean, once *he*—clean-cut, Ivy League–like Jeet—had been arrested for murder himself, and *that* had turned out okay. And once he'd been—or so I thought—kidnapped, and *that* had turned out all right, too. Given all that, I'd go with the coffee-break assumption, or else that he'd gone home without realizing that it was still my first day in Bead, and I didn't have a clue where home was.

"No, I haven't seen him," DeWitt said, "but when you do, ask him if he'd like a piece on the controversy over at Bucking Hill Cemetery. There's this hot spring practically underneath it and—"

"Don't waste it on *The Bead Weekly*," June DeWitt intervened. "We can go national with that baby. Think big, Boone. Think big. I mean, maybe *American Heritage* would be interested." And then she started explaining to me, "The cemetery is still kept in the traditional Texas manner. The ground is bare, and there are mounds to indicate—"

The last thing in the world I cared about was that cemetery. "Stuff it," I said as I headed out to the parking lot, hoping that the sheriff hadn't yet pulled away.

He hadn't.

He was talking into the radio while Della sat imperiously in the backseat, her eyes as hard as beads. A substantial wire screen ensured that she would stay there, unable to reach and/or harm the arresting officer.

"One thing," I said to the sheriff. "I need to ask her just one thing."

"Ask away, little lady. Ask away."

So I leaned in while he ducked and I asked if she had any idea where Jeet might be.

And of course, while I was waiting for her to answer, my mind did an evil thing and allowed me to briefly envision Jeet's battered body in the Dumpster behind which I'd parked Tiny's car.

Della looked at me as if she didn't even know who Jeet was.

"Della," I pleaded, "at least tell me that you didn't hurt him."

"Hurt him!" she spat. "He hurt me! Seeing that woman, night after night. Announcing he would leave me. He hurt me!"

Those were the intelligible words, and none of them were about Jeet. A lot of gibberish followed.

"You have another question?" the sheriff asked me.

"Well, I was wondering if she wanted me to call anybody."

"We'll take care of that," he said. Then his voice shifted into something you'd have to call kindly. "The lady isn't in a condition to talk about such things now. Matter of fact, she's about to go into something called a fugue state."

"A fugue state?"

"I presented a paper on it at a law-enforcement seminar in Austin just the other day. We'll have a counselor on hand back at the station to deal with her. A trauma specialist."

A counselor? In Bead? A law-enforcement seminar? Him? Did that mean he wasn't just some podunk sheriff?

"By the way," the sheriff said, lowering his voice. "Towns Loving would have covered that seminar, if you know what I mean. Your husband, though, he didn't act like it was important. Do you know why that might be?"

"Controversy," Della was shrieking. "That's all Towns Loving cared about. Stirring things up. Stirring people up."

I shrugged. "I'll tell Jeet about it," I said, but the sheriff was not placated.

"Should have guessed he wouldn't know diddly," the sheriff went on. "I mean, the boy couldn't find the proper light switch in the rental car he was driving. Couldn't turn the goddamn lights off. Yup. Should have told me something."

I nodded in appreciation of the man's memory. But hey, so what if Jeet is not a rocket scientist when it comes to cars? And so what if he didn't think much of the crime beat? *He's a food critic,* I wanted to shout. *He's a food critic at the Austin paper.*

But with this sheriff, I somehow didn't think it would help. So I smiled. Helplessly. Furiously. And asked if he knew where Jeet might be.

The sheriff looked at his watch. "Nope. Don't have a clue where that boy is at this time of the evening," the sheriff said, starting the car and gunning the engine.

In the backseat, Della continued babbling. She

was back to speaking in tongues. Then she had a lucid moment and she focused on me.

"Could you bring my curling iron?" she asked.

The sheriff shook his head no. "She can't have that where she's going," he said. Then he lost all trace of sympathy and lapsed back into redneckery. "Yep." He spat out the window onto the ground. "When it comes to news coverage, we sure do miss old Towns."

Another vehicle appeared. A van with SHERIFF painted on the side.

"They'll be videotaping your statement now," the sheriff said.

"My what?"

The sheriff sort of laughed. "Just like I said. Tell the boys with the cameras and the microphones what you know about what went on."

"From when to when?"

"From whenever to whenever." He shook his head as if dealing with the biggest dunce in North America.

I stood there and watched as the two of them—the sheriff and Della—whizzed away.

Oooh, I thought as I waited for the sheriff's minions to set up their equipment. Ooooh.

I wanted to defend Jeet's editorial practices, whatever they were. But the sheriff hadn't given me even half a chance.

And he probably *did* know where Jeet hung out.

Oooh. I paced around on the pavement, seething. So where, exactly, did that leave me?

"We're ready for your statement," a very young deputy said.

And I turned toward the camera and found a smile forming on my face as I recounted, for the official record, my day.

*   *   *

When I was done, I directed the deputy to the side door.

Through the lighted window I could see the figures of the folks who were still inside. I sure as hell didn't want to go back in there. But I didn't have to, because shortly Tiny was standing near her car, obviously waiting for me.

"Listen," she said, "I think I'm going to take a certain someone up on his offer. You know. To board Coronado at his place?"

"Oh." She meant Booger, I thought.

"So if you could come home with me, maybe we can take him there in your horse trailer?"

"You mean now?" Right. She locks me up inside her travel trailer, accuses me of trying to steal her horse, and now wants me to cart said animal all over Bead?

"Okay," I said. "But I really do have to find my husband."

"Oh," Tiny said. "Booger had to go home and get ready to go to work. But he said he knew where Jeet would be in—" she peered at her wristwatch— "about two hours."

"Okay," I said. "But if we could kind of take the long way back, I could, like, maybe see if I see him someplace?"

"If you want," she said.

I don't know how long we cruised the streets of Bead, but we saw absolutely nothing—like the car he'd been driving, for instance—to indicate that he'd been there.

I mean nada.

Up and down we cruised, kind of zigging up one block and zagging down another, all the while kind of generally making our way toward Tiny's place. I didn't know whether or not it was an effective search pattern, the kind you'd use if you were looking for, say, a downed airplane, but it sure didn't yield anything.

Jeet.

I wished I'd had a bullhorn so that I could shout his name.

Finally, Tiny said, "I think we ought to give it up."

"Okay."

And we were off to the sorry farm where the horse was housed.

I was curious, I have to admit, about seeing the horse close up.

I mean, if you're like me, you've seen famous horses on videotape, seen their pictures in magazines, maybe even seen them at horse shows from afar.

That pales when you're within petting distance.

Because the superachieving horses are breathtaking, usually.

They're bigger, for one thing, than you ever think they're going to be. And they're sassier. It's as if they know all about the acclaim they've received and they never doubt for one moment that they deserve it.

I kept wanting to prepare for seeing Coronado, and I thought the best way to do that would be to ask Tiny questions about him—about how long she'd had him, how she'd trained him, problems she'd had. But that could wait until we got to her place.

Then we were there.

Coronado was an Andalusian cross, it turned out, which didn't surprise me. Although after the article blaming Tiny for Sebastian Keyes's wreck had appeared she'd lost everything else, she'd managed—just barely—to hang on to the horse.

"Thanks to Brian, I'll never have to worry about losing Coronado again," Tiny said.

"Brian?" I asked. Had I missed someone in all of this?

"Booger." She laughed. "His real name is Brian."

"Oh." Who'd have guessed.

"But are you just going to live here in Bead? Stop showing? Stop teaching?" I asked.

"I don't know," she said. "I can't see myself attracting any clients right now. And even if I could, I think I kind of like it here in Bead."

She did?

There was a long pause. And then she said, "I knew Brian, way back when. When I was a little girl, I mean. He had a young gelding and he let me ride him. He was responsible for . . . well, my career, I guess."

A young gelding who'd grown into an old gelding in Booger's care. And all the while he'd carried this torch for Tiny, too. It was touching beyond belief.

But meanwhile there was Jeet. "Let's roll, okay?" I said. "I've got a husband to find."

We wrapped Coronado as if we were about to ship him overseas, but I didn't care. I always err on the side of caution myself, leg wraps, tail wrap, head bumper. The whole enchilada. I was glad to see that she did, too.

And the horse walked into the trailer as if he'd done it every day.

"He's really well trained," I said.

"I should hope so." She laughed. "I mean, I used to make my living that way."

We pulled out, inching over the heavily rutted drive.

I said, "You could probably do it from here," meaning that people would drive a couple of hours for a decent dressage lesson. It was true. I'd done it myself, and a lot of my friends still did, some trailering from Austin to practically Houston on a weekly basis.

"That's what I want to do," she said. "But you don't know what it's like, having people accuse you of something in print like that. Having to defend yourself. Having people . . ." Here she paused and made a sort of puffing sound. The sound of new-found cynicism. "Having people believe the worst anyway, no matter what you say or what you did until that point."

"Towns was going to correct all that?" I asked.

"He wanted to. He was a good man." She went on to tell me how he'd won her trust almost instantly. How, when she'd told him about the tacky newspaper article that had all but destroyed her, he'd set about, right away, to make things right. "I'm sure he would have, too," she said.

"And you weren't having an affair with him."

"Of course not," she said.

And I believed her. I mean, if Booger—I mean Brian—was the kind of man she went for, she would hardly have been impressed by Towns's tweedy type.

"God," I said. "Don't you wonder how a guy as nice as Towns ended up with a bitch like Della?"

We were both quiet, thinking about it. But stranger things have happened. There will always be all-out bitches who can pour the syrup at exactly the right moment so that the man they're after won't see.

Like that ancient movie, *All About Eve*.

"She was very pretty," Tiny said at last.

"Want to stop for your mail?" I asked her when I saw the battered mailbox at the driveway's end.

"I hardly ever get mail," she said.

"Oh, come on."

I pulled Mother up beside the box, and she leaned out, opened it, and cocked her head to the left when she looked inside. She reached in and extracted a manila envelope.

She opened it, pulled out a sheaf of papers.

Then she burst into an enormous smile, a smile that seemed too big for a face as small as hers. She waved the papers in my face, and then scooted across the broad front seat so we could more or less read it together.

"It's Towns's article," she said. "I wonder how long it's been sitting there."

I opened Mother's door to get the overhead light to come on and said, "Oooh, listen," and together we proceeded to read the story of Tiny's great vindication.

"Where'd he send it?" I asked.

"His cover letter's right here," she said. "Oh, God. It's to *Vanity Fair*. And listen, it mentions the other two papers—the tabloids that dumped all over me—by name."

"And he tells all about the television exec who distorted that tape on *Sharp Copy*," I noted. "And he names the one who had the chance to run the whole tape, the real tape, and wouldn't."

"And—oh, this is great. Keyes is still paralyzed, but he's able to talk now, and look! Even *he* says that none of the accusations were true."

"When this comes out," I said, "you'll have your life back."

Tiny sighed. "I don't know," she said. "I still think maybe my life is here."

"You mean you really do like Booger?" I asked. She, who had hung around with the likes of Sebastian Keyes?

"Brian," she said. "And yes. I think he's wonderful."

* * *

"Uh, well, uh . . ."

"And he has the bluest eyes," she went on. Sort of dreamily, too.

We got to Boog—Brian's, and he was standing there in the yard as though he'd been keeping vigil, waiting for us to arrive. The enclosure where Plum and Spier stood waiting was flooded with light from a halogen up on a tall wooden pole.

Jeez. A lighted arena yet. I hadn't even noticed that this morning, but then, why would I have? He was ready for Tiny all right. She could easily give lessons out there in what looked like daylight.

He came smiling and helped unload Coronado, and reverse the wrapping procedure that Tiny and I had applied. He seemed to know what he was doing, too. He even rerolled the wraps, tucking up the ends with practiced efficiency.

I planned to stay there only long enough to watch the horses schmoozing over the cross fence, but even so, I had taken note of a curious fact:

Boog—Brian—*did* have the bluest eyes.

Plum and Spier ran around when they saw Coronado and then pretty soon they were nose to nose over the cross fence.

They'd sniff and then they'd squeal and then they'd run away, bucking and farting. Then they'd make another approach.

But you knew they'd all be buddies pretty quick.

And anyway, even if they hated each other, I'd be moving them back home pretty quick. Like that night if I was lucky, but certainly in the morning.

Because without Jeet and without Della, *The Bead Weekly* would go belly up pretty quick.

Poor Towns, I thought. It was as though everything he'd put himself into had come undone.

But just hanging out near the horses made me feel a hundred percent better.

And you know why. Because sometimes just being around a horse can make the gloom you are feeling go away.

If you have horses, you know exactly what I mean. It's as though they exude something, like . . . natural Prozac, maybe. The act of running a currycomb around and around and around releases a serotoninlike substance that we inhale. And I don't care if this isn't scientifically proven. I don't care, because it's true.

Anyway, Tiny watched along with me and then she said, "They are fine animals, your horses."

"I'm glad you got to see them," I told her. "Because I'm pretty sure I'll be out of here in the morning, if I can find my husband."

Brian frowned. "Wait a minute. Are you talking about that Jeet fellow, new guy in town? Has a hank of hair that either hangs down like this"—he clapped a hand over one side of his forehead—"or else kind of sticks up?"

"That's Jeet!" I said.

"Likes to eat?"

"Yup."

"Well." Brian looked at his watch. "I got to get to work. But I'll tell you where that man of yours might be, oh, reckon an hour or so from now."

"Where's that?"

And when he told me, I knew he had to be right.

<u>CHAPTER</u> 13

I waved good-bye and toddled away with a real sense of purpose. But part of me was afraid that Jeet, being a newspaperman, wouldn't want to leave once he'd heard all the news.

Because, think about it, there was so much!

Della.

The movie.

The cemetery thing.

In my mind's eye, I could see the front page, all three stories arranged there for the reader's perusal. Oh, and of course the one about the horses rescuing me from Tiny's travel trailer, that was four.

I could even see photographs, like the one that Boone DeWitt had taken, gracing the front page. That and maybe Della at the funeral, if someone had one, or even Della at her wedding to Towns, or Della as Miss Macon. There were probably extant photos like that.

So would Jeet be seduced by them? Seduced into small-town newspapering?

I hoped not.

Because my day in Bead felt more like a month, maybe even a year. All I wanted was to sit down with Lola and Jeet and talk about all that had gone on.

The movie people, for instance. The actors who looked like Kevin Costner and Clint Eastwood. I could imagine Lola doing a number on that.

Not that I couldn't live in Bead if that's what Jeet decided to do. I mean, with Tiny here, it wasn't the equestrian wasteland that it appeared to be when we'd first talked about coming.

That had to count for something.

So maybe Jeet and I could make a go of it here, and he could take up where Townsend Loving had left off, the fierce crusading small-town editor, the man who asks no quarter and gives none, the man who fights for truth, justice, and the American way.

Yeah.

And just to keep his hand in, food-wise, Jeet could publish a new recipe in the paper every week.

And me, I could officiate—as Jeet's wife, of course—at ribbon cuttings and such. Something I was sure that Della had never done.

Della. Phew. It gave me the willies.

Of course, if I suspected Jeet was having an affair, I'd be pretty upset, too. I don't think I'd aim Mother at him, though, no matter what.

Anyway, while my mind was churning thus, I saw him yet again: Tony Perkins. He was standing on the side of the road, waving frantically.

At me!

I thought, Hey! Another story maybe. Like, what's it like to go through life looking like a famous movie star who just happens to have portrayed one of the most heinous killers ever?

Norman Bates.

Mama's boy extraordinaire.

So I pulled Mother onto the shoulder of the road

to see what it was that Tony Perkins needed from *moi*.

"Hi!" I said, rolling the window down and feeling around the seat for my reporter's pad. I wrote *Tony Perkins* on a fresh page and extended my hand.

I was very high up, being in Mother and all, and so I had to stretch halfway out of Mother's window in order to shake the man's hand. "Could I interview you?" I said. "I mean, just for a minute. Because I'm on my way to—ouch!"

I had managed to clasp Perkins's hand with my own, but instead of shaking it, he yanked, so that I not only dropped the notebook, but was almost wrenched through the window of the truck. "Hey," I said, jerking back inside. "That hurt."

I almost had a mind not to do a story at all, except that he seemed bent on it. In fact, he was opening the door to Mother and reaching up for me.

"Hold it," I said. "I can understand why you'd be excited about . . ." That was when I saw the knife.

It was a huge knife, too. A cleaver, practically. Or at least it looked that way in the gathering night.

"Look," I tried, but something about the way his eyes were glittering made me abandon the sentence before I could even form it in my mind.

But what was he going to do? Hack me to death on the side of the highway?

I considered my options. Like, I could gun Mother while he still had his feet on the pavement there and probably knock him down in the process.

Then I could back over him, smash him dead.

Except that I didn't really want to do something like that.

Plus I'm not that good in reverse and would probably miss.

And then he'd get me anyway, only he'd be madder than he was right now.

I decided to forget about the backing, just gun Mother and get out of Dodge (no pun intended), but it didn't work out that way, because while I was going back and forth and back and forth in my mind, he hoisted himself up and was now shoving the knife toward my cheek and saying, "Get out."

A carjacking! Right here in Bead.

"Okay, I'll get out," I said, "but there are a couple of things you should know about the transmission before you—"

Except he was back on the pavement again and this time he had yanked me out with him.

But of course. Because what was he going to do? Climb over me and squoosh himself beneath the steering wheel, too?

I stepped back so that he would have easy access to the truck, which was rumbling healthily away.

He grabbed my arm. "Oh, no you don't," he said.

"Oh, right. The transmission. Well, you have to make sure that if you're going into reverse, you shift into reverse before you come to a stop, because otherwise, she'll grind and you'll have to—"

"Walk," he said, shoving me forward.

He was giving up on Mother, just like that.

"No, really," I said, "It's easy once you—"

"Walk!" he said more forcefully.

"Well, look," I told him, "I should at least shut the ignition off, because otherwise I'll run out of gas."

He waved the knife at me. "You making fun of me?" he asked.

"Good God, no," I said. Why should he think such a thing? Was he crazy or something?

So we walked.

My feet began to hurt, and meanwhile it got totally dark as opposed to the partially dark that it had been. I mean pitch. Except that just when I thought that, a pretty bright moon emerged from a thick formation of clouds.

The summer solstice. The longest day of the year—and I'd attest to that, all right—was *finis*.

"Where are we going?" I asked.

"My place," he said.

We turned up the road to the cemetery.

Oh, God. The house behind the Bates Motel.

"Don't you have a car?" I asked him.

"They took my license away," he said, "after my release."

I didn't want to know what zoo that might have been from. Still, my mouth kept moving despite my resolve. "You were released?" I asked.

"It was close," he said, "but, yeah."

"From . . . ?"

"You know very well from where. Because that husband of yours did a story on it."

"Jeet?"

He flashed the knife some more. "Don't get funny," he said.

"Jeet is my husband," I said. "The only husband I've ever had. You must mean Towns."

"Towns. That's right."

"Then you want Della," I said. "Not me."

"You're Della," he insisted.

"Am not," I said.

"Are, too," he countered.

Under ordinary circumstances, this might have been flattering. I mean Della was a babe. "Take a better look," I said, admitting defeat.

"Don't have a light," he said. "Have to wait till we get home."

Good. He'd see then. He'd see that my figure, not to mention my face, was not in the Miss Anything category. Phew. I'd be home free.

I felt easy enough to try a little joke. "Hey," I said, "your hobby isn't taxidermy, is it?"

He stopped and looked up at the moon. He addressed an unknown someone up there. "She's seen the movie," he said. "She knows what it is I've got to do."

So we walked the rest of the way in silence. Because I *had* seen the movie, of course.

God, I even knew the score. By which I mean the music. At least the very distinctive manic slasher music that they played when Janet Leigh got iced in the shower.

I could hear the music now.

And the thing is, I think he could, too.

He picked up the pace. "You hear that, don't you?" he asked.

He seemed upset.

Upset was not, under the circumstances, a desirable state.

We came around a bend in the road and saw it: the house, the barren mounds before it. It looked like a Charles Addams cartoon.

Except that the music was definitely in full swing, and there was a huge Rolls-Royce parked in front of the place.

"Karston!" my would-be attacker exclaimed. And took off.

I stood there and pondered my options.

Walking back to Mother was not one of them. I would be overtaken somewhere along the road. And anyway, when I got to Mother, she would likely have run out of gas.

Plus, it was a far piece we'd walked, Norman Bates and I.

I would have to depend on whoever was inside the house for rescue.

Unless of course the keys were in the Rolls. Then it would merely be another foray into grand theft auto, and hey. I'd be safe.

I pulled myself into the Rolls.

No keys.

But have you ever been inside a Rolls? We're talking luxury. Luxury so stunning that you might, even under circumstances such as these, pause.

Especially since there just might be a telephone inside the thing.

And there was one, tucked under the dash in its very own little holder.

There was just one problem.

Directions hadn't been included with the thing.

I punched every button I could see and I never managed to raise a dial tone.

Which reminded me of the bottle of Gatorade somehow.

And of *Richard III*, which we read in Honors English where I'd first laid eyes on Jeet. Richard, saying, "I am too childish foolish for this world."

Silly, how the mind under stress can work.

Except it made me realize this:

I'd survived a hell of a lot within perhaps a twelve-hour period. So what was I afraid of now? Of Tony Perkins? When I had a Rolls-Royce owner inside to protect me, carry me to safety, as it were?

No. I was anything but too childish foolish for

this world. I was *in charge* of this world. This world was mine.

I strode manfully up to the house, whence the music from *Psycho* still seemed to pour.

Once in the vestibule, I could hear that an argument was in full swing.

Kat Karston was yelling, "But we'll pay you the standard location fee."

Norman Bates was having none of it. "No," he said. He stood in the center of the room, arms crossed, and looking very proprietary.

His knife was not in evidence.

Nonetheless, I didn't feel as though butting in would be the perfect thing.

"Then I'll go," Karston said. "I can't negotiate with someone as limited as you seem to be."

"Good." Bates waved him away. "Go."

I backed out of the room and eased my way toward the Rolls with every intention of hurling myself unbidden into the broad backseat.

I felt like shouting hallelujah. I was soon to be outta there. Outta there and back to Bead.

I never thought I'd look forward to it.

But I wasn't counting on Karston's anger and the speed with which it propelled him.

Which is to say that he overtook me about five feet shy of the mark.

"Oh, Jesus," he said. "You."

I smiled brightly. "That's right. It's me."

He smirked and pushed past me.

Or tried to. I caught his sleeve. "Listen," I whispered. "I need a ride back into town."

"Oh." He glowered at me. "Do you?"

"Look," I said, "there's been a lot of water under the bridge. But this nutcase here"—I gestured toward the house where Bates held court—"has been holding me prisoner. He let me go when he saw your car."

"Oh." Karston's tone changed into something silky. "You do need a ride back to town, then."

I got in.

He started the Rolls. He hit a button and the windows rolled shut. Then an almost imperceptible blower began to cool the interior. The car had a sealed feel to it, kind of like a tomb.

I laughed, partly with relief. "It's a far cry, your air conditioner, from the throbbing heart of the universe over at the newspaper." And then I proceeded to tell him about Della going bonkers in the offices of *The Bead Weekly* and confessing to having run her husband over.

I must admit, I played up my role in unmasking her, and turned it into, you know, a sort of joke on the rubes in Bead. I mean, after all, Karston was a Hollywood guy, and I was practically from Austin.

I was really whooping it up. You know how it is with something this over-the-top. You can turn it into a pretty funny schtick.

Except that Karston didn't laugh. "And where is Della now?" he asked.

"The sheriff took her," I said. "To jail, I guess."

"Is that so." He pulled the car to a stop and drummed his fingers against the steering wheel.

I felt something, I don't know. Probably the kind of sixth-sense warning thing that the women who decided *not* to go with Ted Bundy felt.

"I'll get out here," I said. "I don't mind." And without giving him any time to respond, I opened the door and was out.

The air was moist, but it felt womblike with its welcome. I still didn't know why. I only knew that I was far enough away from the hulking Bates house not to feel that Norman—Tony Perkins—was still a threat. And I could breathe out here, whereas trapped inside that Rolls, I'd begun to feel I couldn't.

And maybe Kat Karston felt the very same way, because, *brrrrrt,* the window on the passenger side was whirring down.

"I'd like to show you something," he said, stopping and getting out.

I saw something in his hand.

And a little voice inside me was saying, *Oh, no.*

But it wasn't a weapon of any kind. It was a flashlight.

He led me to the hood of the car. Shone the light on the lady that was the hood ornament. "Take a good look," he said.

I squinted. "What?" I asked.

"Does it look familiar?" he asked back.

"Well, I've never seen a Rolls before," I said.

He laughed. "Look again." He shone the light on the hood again, and I squinted at it once more.

My God.

It was Della. Naked, or nearly so. Her hourglass figure wore only a banner. I squinted at it. MISS MACON, it read.

"Great workmanship," I tried.

He laughed again. "Yes. I had it made with the first year's proceeds at the restaurant."

"The restaurant?"

"Smokers. It's mine. The place is a gold mine."

"The restaurant made more money than your movies?" I asked.

"The restaurant finances them," he said.

"But what about this Della thing?" I gestured at the hood ornament.

"Della and I are lovers," he said. "This ornament was our private joke. Our way of proclaiming it to the world."

"Without the world actually noticing," I said.

"That's right."

Cool. Except how did this concern me?

"It seemed fitting, then, that we should use this car."

"Use it for what?" I asked.

"To kill Towns."

"You were with her?" I squealed. "When she ran him down?"

"No. I was behind her. I saw what she tried to do, but in the end she lost her nerve. She kind of nudged him with her car and knocked him down. I came along and finished the job."

"But she's been arrested," I said. "Plus this car isn't dented or anything."

"She's been arrested thanks to you," he said. "And as far as the car goes, I took it to the body shop in Houston the next morning."

I thought: There will be records, maybe even pictures. Body shops do that sometimes. I said: "Well, actually, she got herself arrested. But anyway, why tell me about your own involvement? I mean, aren't you afraid I'll talk?"

"Are you suggesting that I'd let poor Della take the fall for this?" he asked, his eyes blazing and his breath coming hard. I could practically hear his heart beating.

"No," I said. "No way. You wouldn't, I know." My heart was drowning his out. I could feel sweat pouring out of me, although you'd think that, at this point, I'd be used to talking to crazy people.

"No," he said, his voice flattening out and growing calm again. "You won't be able to talk."

"Why not?"

"Because you'll be dead."

CHAPTER 14

How do these things happen to me? It can't be karma, because I'm a relatively nice person. So why do I always find myself in situations that I'd rather not be in?

Like this one. With some half-baked, third-rate Hollywood director—of Christian vampire movies, yet—telling me I'm going to be dead.

And implying that he's going to be the one to bring that circumstance about.

Except that, unlike Norman Bates, he didn't have a weapon. I mean, what was he going to do? Throttle me with his bare hands? Who did he think he was?

"We'll see about that," I said, turning sharply in the direction of town.

He remained behind, in stunned silence, I guess.

And I strode on at a good clip, fueled by the adrenaline that was pumping through my system. My anger pushed a series of disparaging epithets through my mind, things like "jerk" and "bum" and "weenie" and, well, every bad word I could think of.

Until I heard the sound of his engine revving in the background. Then I knew what his intention was.

My God.

He was going to run me down.

The way he had run down Towns.

I guess my life was flashing before my eyes, because I kept thinking of my old gym teacher, Miss Barr, who, bless her heart, was obsessed with the notion that someone was out to abduct her or worse.

But this came in handy sometimes, because she'd given our gym class a list of self-defense measures. Self-defense measures that, *mirabile dictu,* had stood me—and often—in fine stead.

The one I was about to employ was simple and nonviolent. It consisted of going in the direction opposite to the direction of the car that was in pursuit.

I mean, think about it. You're walking down the road and some sleaze pulls up beside you, right? Well, you want to run like the dickens in the opposite direction, because then he has to take the time to turn around to chase you.

Easy, huh?

Except for one thing.

Kat wasn't trying to scoop me up. He was trying to mow me down.

Nonetheless, I used the Barr method at the very last minute and managed to foil him somewhat.

Except that he came around quite nicely for a second pass.

Well, as I said, my life was passing before my eyes. Because now I was thinking about my riding teacher, Wanda. Back home, I mean, pre-Bead.

This may strike you as a non sequitur, but believe me, it's not. Because Wanda believed in something called "imaging."

In imaging you are, in your mind's eye, someone else. Your clunky body becomes, oh, I don't know, the sylphlike body of Nicole Uphoff. Or—to be more true to my own body type—Robert Dover.

Except that in this case, I didn't want to be a

rider. I wanted to be a horse. I wanted to run and jump like some steeplechaser.

But all I could think of was Cigar, the horse who had won the Woodward without so much as breaking a sweat. The horse who was Horse of the Year.

Okay, I was Cigar, with a huge, comfy stride. Cigar, my mane flying, my neck straining toward the wire and the win. I was Cigar, leaping over the grave mounds in my way, and listening as the car that was chasing me slalomed around them as best it could.

I was doing okay, heading—well, I wasn't sure where. I mean, I didn't want to end up back at Norman Bates's place, right? But heading off into the night, maybe to a grove of mesquite, where Kat Karston wouldn't be able to follow.

And then I saw a second set of headlights coming from the direction of the highway.

Oh, God. If Karston had an accomplice, I was dead, cooked, finito, fried.

Meanwhile Karston was tearing up the graveyard in pursuit of me, clumps of brown dirt ripping the night air, wheels a-spin.

Then a wrenching sound. I looked back and saw Karston's car hung up on a particularly large grave mound, all four of its wheels in the air.

"You stupid . . ." His voice was muffled, but I understood that much of what he said.

Then there was the brief growl of a siren and the sheriff came to a stop between Karston's car and me.

"What in tarnation's going on?" he asked, bellying out of the car to where I, un-Cigarlike, was huffing, trying to catch my breath.

"He was"—I took a pause to breathe—"ch-chasing me."

The sheriff looked in the direction I'd pointed,

where Kat Karston's car, Della hood ornament and all, rocked unsteadily on its ghoulish perch.

"You mean Chester?"

"Kat Karston," I repeated. "The director."

"Chester," the sheriff spat. "He's a hometown boy. Owns that restaurant out by the road. Smokers."

"He was having an affair with Della," I said. "Evidently he was really the one who mowed Towns down."

"That what he said?"

"Yes."

"Kind of jibes with what Della told me."

"Except wait a minute," I said. "If Della was having an affair, why was she so worried about Towns and Tiny?"

"Projection," the sheriff said. "That's the psychological term for it. I'm going to be giving a workshop on the subject in Austin next week, so this example will come in handy. I don't suppose your editor husband will be covering it, though. Probably thinks it ain't important enough. He'd rather be covering the Yard of the Week."

I sighed.

The sheriff patted his holster. "Well," he said, "guess I'll go pick up Chester."

"Where is he?" I asked, suddenly afraid. "Isn't he still in the car?"

"Nope. He's gone on down the road, I reckon."

"Wait a minute," I said. "I don't exactly want to be left alone."

"Go on up to the house," the sheriff said, pointing at Norman Bates's place looming on the horizon. I'd been heading toward it unwittingly after all.

"Are you kidding? That Tony Perkins look-alike brought me out here at knifepoint."

The sheriff laughed. "Well, I saw you had written

his name on that little notepad. Which reminds me, I ought to give you a ticket, leaving that rig of yours practically in the middle of the road. I even had to shut the engine off."

"I'm telling you," I insisted, "I was abducted."

The sheriff looked at the Bates house and shook his head indulgently. "That boy is harmless," he said. "It kind of went to his head, people making remarks about Tony Perkins and Norman Bates all the time. The boy has watched that there movie *Psycho* probably every day of his grown-up life. Even bought the sequel to it, I hear."

The sequel is where Tony Perkins stutters out the word "cc-ccc-cu-cutlery." I mentioned that Mr. Harmless had been wielding some.

"Retractable blade." The sheriff laughed even more. "I swear it. If he'd have tried to stab you, you'd have known."

"Yes, but . . ."

The sheriff put a fatherly hand on my shoulder. "Bead's a small town," he said. "You gotta make allowances for people's idiosyncrasies."

Sure enough, Chester, aka Kat, was hiking back toward Bead. The sheriff pulled up alongside. "Chester? Looks like the jig is up," he said.

Chester kept walking.

The sheriff kept cruising, kind of like a shark. "Chester? Bead proper is a pretty fair piece away."

Still nothing.

"Chester?" the sheriff tried again. "I think Della could use some company."

Chester stopped. Opened the rear door. Got inside.

The sheriff clicked the locks and looked at me, sitting in the passenger seat beside him. I was glad for that thick screen between Karston and me. "Psychology," he said. "You gotta use it. That's what my dissertation is called. *Psychology and Its Myriad Law-Enforcement Applications*. Gonna do a talk show on that puppy one day next week. Oprah's people have called and I got the plane ticket to Chicago and all. They're putting me up in a fancy hotel and feeding me and stuff."

Did they sell chicken-fried steak in Chicago? I wondered. But I didn't ask. Instead I said, "When you did absolutely zip at the newspaper—you know, when Della was doing her X-Acto knife thing—was that psychology, too?"

I was still a little ticked about that.

"Did that one by the book," the sheriff said. "Hostage situation. Innocent person at risk. What was I supposed to do? If I'd have jumped Della, she'd have stuck Tiny with that blade for sure. And anyway, I got the whole of it on tape."

The sheriff pulled up alongside Mother. He looked at his watch. "If you're still looking for your husband, now's the time you can find him at—"

"I know," I interrupted.

<u>CHAPTER</u> 15

I walked into Smokers and adjusted my eyesight to the haze. There, in the corner booth where he and I had lunched, sat Jeet. He—if the local wisdom that I'd heard expressed from just about everyone in town was true—had arrived there precisely fourteen minutes earlier.

I walked up, expecting, I don't know, the sort of welcome a person who has had a day like mine deserved.

Jeet spotted me, smiled, stood up, and enveloped me in his arms. "I was just about to go looking for you," he said. "But I figured you were with your horses."

Welcome approved. Except that I squeezed back harder than I'd planned to because, truth be told, I'm not really as tough as I seem. I mean, tough is what rises to get me out of scrapes, but deep down inside, I'm a weenie.

Jeet seemed surprised. But also pleased.

"Jeet," I said, "Della's—"

"—outrageous," he finished for me, even though that wasn't at all what I was going to say. "Firing me like that. I should have known."

"Firing you!" That suddenly seemed worse than her having attempted to murder Towns and later Tiny.

"It all started at the wedding, you know," Jeet told me.

"At the wedding? What wedding?"

"Theirs," Jeet said, sinking down onto his seat in a way that suggested deep discouragement.

"Whose?"

"Towns and Della's," he said.

"What happened at the wedding?" I asked, remembering that Jeet and Towns had hardly spoken, but not remembering much of anything else about it.

"Oh, never mind." Jeet waved his hand dismissively. "It's probably crazy to still be holding a grudge. Except that I never wanted to be. It just surfaced once I was here in Bead."

"What surfaced?"

"The grudge."

"The grudge about . . ." I led him, I hoped, toward completion of the sentence.

"It's not important."

"No," I whined. "I want to know."

"It seems stupid to talk about it now," he said. "Except that, what with Della actually *firing* me . . ." He trailed off.

Which was when I remembered that Karston had said Jeet was fired. I should have wondered right then and there what his relationship with Della was, his being able to do that. Except I'd thought it an idle threat at the time. I mean, at the time, I sure didn't think Del would *dare* fire Jeet, because then where would she be?

But anyway.

"It was right after we'd arrived at the reception," Jeet said. "I congratulated Towns, and he made some remark about how bad he felt that I hadn't done nearly as well as he had. At first I thought he meant—well, you know, that you weren't a

beauty queen like what's-her-face, and I was ready
to deck him for it, except that it turned out . . ." He
gulped right here, as though it was hard for him to
finish.

"Go on," I urged. I felt a little miffed at this point,
too, maybe because of what had been Jeet's first assumption. But then I smiled at the thought of Jeet
decking Towns—or anyone.

"It turned out he meant that I was just a food
writer," Jeet said, "and he was going on to be an editor."

"Big deal," I said. "Look what he was the editor of."

Except that, yes, he had been a good one, apparently, but still.

"Jeet," I said, rubbing his hand and looking into
his eyes as hard and as earnestly as I've ever looked
into anyone's. "You write about food, yes, but you
write about it brilliantly. That's why a New York
publisher wants you to do a book about food. And
anyway, don't you remember that thing you read at
Writer's Harvest?"

I meant that Share Our Strength reading that
writers do all over the country to benefit the home-
less. Jeet had been asked to participate in Austin
the year before and he'd read an absolutely beauti-
ful passage about just what Towns had been disparaging: writing about food.

He looked a little less glum, so I pressed on.

"It was that M.F.K. Fisher thing," I reminded
him, and he actually brightened, remembering.

"It was from *The Gastronomical Me*," he said.

"That's right," I comforted him.

Jeet had memorized the passage, and it was all
about how people criticized her—M.F.K. Fisher—for
writing about food instead of stuff that they—the
people—considered important.

And her answer was that we have these three

basic needs, for food and for security and for love, and they're all kind of mixed up together.

So that when you write about one of them, you're really writing about the other two as well.

I said all that now.

"You remembered," Jeet said.

"Of course I remembered. Jeet, everybody who was there that night will remember. You were—you *are*—wonderful."

He was beaming, with Della and Towns's criticism of what he did for a living all washed clean from his mind.

Which was just as well. It was pretty obvious that my husband wouldn't know a hard news story if it jumped up and bit off his nose.

But we all have our strong points and our weak. What was strong for Jeet was very strong indeed, and what was weak was—well, suffice it to say that he hadn't a clue about anything that had gone on since my arrival in Bead.

And I wondered where to begin and even if I ought to. But I had to eventually, because I couldn't keep him from finding out.

It would be like this story someone told me once about a woman whose husband really liked Elvis Presley, so she tried to keep him from hearing about it when Elvis died. Except that of course she couldn't, and when he found out that his wife had tried to hide it, he got mad and divorced her.

Well, okay, it's not a great story, but you know what I mean: Jeet would eventually hear about Della being arrested, and Karston having come along behind her and really doing the deed.

And he'd find out about the other news, too.

How the cemetery problem was blowing up into a big-deal incident.

How the sheriff was apparently some world-renowned figure in the field of law enforcement.

How some toad had practically made a housing project grind to a halt.

He'd find out about . . . well, everything anyone even moderately news-oriented would have, eventually.

But I don't know. That just made me love Jeet all the more.

Jeet was looking at his watch. "You want an omelette?" he asked me. "It's time."

"Sure." I wondered what checking the time had to do with it, though. So I asked him.

"The cook that I was telling you about—the one I've been coaching—will be here at ten. It's about that now."

He stood up. "Let me go back into the kitchen and round him up and tell him to make two." He started back toward the swinging doors in the rear and then he turned. "I was planning to do a story about him. Now, though . . ."

Right.

"Still, I'd like to get the recipe for the sauce he makes."

Leave it to my husband to be thinking about food. I'm sure that even if I'd begun to tell him about Della, or about my ordeal inside Tiny's trailer or with Tony Perkins, or for that matter, with Kat Karston, he'd have done exactly the same thing. Ordered the omelettes and *then* listened.

So I waited until he ordered the omelettes and came back to our table. Then I said, "Listen, Jeet, a lot has happened."

"Damn right," he said. "I'm going to have to add something in the manuscript I turn in that'll take into account the discoveries I've made. I mean, I don't think it should just be confined to the food I've eaten growing up."

"Uh . . ."

"For instance, this sauce that the cook here makes. It's . . ." He paused and made a circle with his thumb and forefinger and kissed his thumbnail.

I could hear the sheriff's voice: Avoidance behavior, it would say.

But then Jeet stopped avoiding.

"Another day and I'd have quit," he said. "I just couldn't have taken it. I mean"—and here he looked guilty for a moment—"Della was a pain in the butt."

I nodded my complete assent.

Still, he added, "I know, I know, she's a widow and all, but you just can't believe what the woman was like."

"I do, Jeet," I said, "because—"

"God," he went on, ignoring my attempt at consolation and empathy, "the stories she wanted me to write! Hanging files at the insurance agency. I don't know how Towns stood it."

"Maybe he ran out in front of a car," I joked lamely. Fortunately, Jeet ignored my attempt to inject levity into what was not at all a situation likely to receive it. But he didn't chastise me. He just went on with his lament.

"Of course," he said, "I can understand how she'd be scraping just to find *anything* to write about," he said. "I mean, nothing ever happens here."

I didn't say anything, mostly because I didn't know how to break in with all I knew. Without making him feel, I don't know, as though he'd missed the boat.

The boat? Heck, he'd missed the fleet!

And he wouldn't let go. "God," he said, "this town is the pits. I don't even know why they'd *have* a paper in the first place."

Because of the murders and the movies and the protests and . . . ? But I didn't say that. I said, "Well, there is this one story that I know of. . . ."

"Oh, God," he said, looking toward the entrance and then sort of scrunching down in his chair. "Oh, God, look who's here."

I swiveled and saw Boone DeWitt walking crisply toward us. Then the Valkyrie swept into the room. They'd tell Jeet about Della, I just knew.

"Jeet," I blurted out, "Della tried to kill Towns. And she was having an affair with some third-rate Hollywood director who grew up here, and he came along behind her and finished up the job."

Jeet ignored me, his entire focus on the advancing elderly pair. June towered over her husband, and so it was easy to be distracted, observing them, wondering . . . you know. But anyway.

"I'm not the editor anymore." Jeet stood and tried to stop the DeWitts' advance. "If you want to do any stories, you'll have to talk to Della Loving. It's her baby now."

The DeWitts both looked at me, as in, *Didn't you tell him?* Then Boone cleared his throat and asked that very question.

"Tell me what?" Jeet asked, looking accusingly my way.

Before I could respond, the kitchen doors whooshed open and who should appear but Booger—Brian—with gorgeously presented omelettes at the ready. Really, one in each hand. They were fluffy looking, garnished with a slice of orange and a sprig of very fresh-looking parsley.

Oh, God, I sound just like Jeet.

"Robin." Jeet was taking the plates from Booger and putting them down on the surface of the table.

"This is Booger. He's the very promising chef I've been telling you about."

Booger winked at me.

"You know that egg dish we call Frog in the Hole?" Jeet was saying. This is where you cut a circle out of a piece of bread and fry the egg inside it. I grew up calling it Hole in the Wall until I met Jeet. "Well, Booger here puts the cut-out circle *over* the yoke and calls it Pirate with a Patch!"

"Really!" I enthused.

"Booger," Jeet demanded. "You've forgotten the sauce."

"No, I ain't," Booger said, reaching into the pocket of his spectacularly stained cook's apron and producing a mason jar with a big handwritten label on the side.

Jeet read the label. "The recipe!" he said.

DeWitt interrupted. "Sonny," he said. "Junie and I are going to buy *The Bead Weekly*. So I won't be deviling you about stories anymore."

But June couldn't resist boasting from the sidelines, "He did place a portion in the *Enquirer*, though."

"A piece, Junie," DeWitt corrected. "A story is called a piece."

"In the *Enquirer*," June, undaunted, said. "And they bought Boone's picture, too."

Of her on top of Della, I guess.

What popped into my head was the little birdlike man who sold the ads. "Who'll sell ads?" I asked, fearing that the guy would soon be jobless.

"Tooter," the DeWitts chorused.

"He's a real ball of fire," June said.

Jeet hadn't heard a word. He looked triumphant. He was still reading what Booger had written. "It's got Worcestershire in it. And beer! Beer! What a master touch!" He looked as though he was about to kiss Booger on the cheek. Then he looked at the DeWitts. "What did you say about the *Enquirer*?"

"Jeet." I put a hand on his shoulder and repeated, enunciating exaggeratedly. "Della killed Towns. Or tried to. Then her boyfriend came along afterward and finished the job."

He had been standing. Now he sort of collapsed into a sitting position. He looked down at his plate.

And I knew he was shocked and maybe even moved, because his gorgeous omelette sat there, congealing on the plate.

DeWitt interrupted. "Did you hear me, sonny? June's going to let me buy *The Bead Weekly*," he said. "She's going to take pictures. And I'm going to get to write. I'm going to start off with that cemetery piece."

Jeet sighed and nodded with an air of resignation. I could see that he was thinking that the paper was doomed. So I didn't spoil things by telling him anything more. A small-town newsman Jeet wasn't cut out to be.

He turned to Booger, who was waiting for him to taste the food he'd prepared. The man—Brian, I mean—was literally rubbing his hands together in expectation. Which meant he cared, a fine quality in a chef.

But I could see that Jeet wasn't thinking about food, which of course was rare. He was hesitant, and I think he was thinking about Townsend Loving, and about their boyhood together in Abilene. He was thinking about dreams and the way they bloom or die or turn hybrid. He was thinking about Della and how he'd never liked her, and now he knew—in a maxed-out version—why.

He shook his head, as if to clear it.

And then he was looking at me in a way that said that amid all of this craziness, there was us and the way we loved each other. Us and our good friends back home. Us and how lucky we were.

Don't ask me how I knew this. I just did.

But the other thing about Jeet is that he's polite.

He lifted the fork to his lips. He inhaled the fragment of omelette thereon. He unscrewed the mason jar and sniffed and poured. He chewed. He smiled. He told Brian he was a wonderful cook.

And all I wanted, then and there, was to be back with him at Primrose Farm, living our regular life.

"Let's finish our omelettes and go get the horses tonight," I said. "Let's go home."